Chasing Shadows

Jason Richards

Published by Whodunit Publishing, 2018.

COPYRIGHT

Copyright © 2018 Jason Richards.

All rights reserved. Without limiting the rights under reserved copyright, no part of this publication may be reproduced, stored in or introduced into a retrieval system, or transmitted, in any form, or by any means (electronic, mechanical, photocopying, recording, or otherwise) without the express written permission of the publisher.

Cover image © Carlos Castilla (carloscastilla). Images used under license from 123RF®. Cover text created using CoolText.com. Cover design by Whodunit Publishing.

This book is a work of fiction. Names, characters, places and incidents are either the product of the author's imagination or are used fictitiously. Any resemblance to persons, living or dead, organizations, events, or locales is entirely coincidental.

CHAPTER 1

JAX AND MIKEY

JAX AND MIKEY DRAGGED the man into the alley. He looked like Rocky Balboa after fifteen rounds with Apollo Creed.

But there would be no credit for going the distance with the heavyweight champ.

Jax and Mikey weren't finished.

The man just wanted the beating to stop.

Jax dropped the man like a stone. The man's arms bending in positions they shouldn't. Mikey got down on his haunches directly in front of the man. He leaned forward and smiled.

"Care to reconsider your position?" Mikey said.

"I can't," the man gurgled.

"That is unfortunate," Mikey said. He stood and turned to his brother.

"Okay, Jax, finish him."

"No loose ends," Jax said to Mikey.

"Never leave loose ends," replied Mikey.

Jax stepped forward, bent over, and picked the man up by his collar. He tossed him like a rag doll against the building. The man slammed against the brick resembling a test crash dummy. He slumped to the ground. Jax moved toward the motionless man and pulled him up again. The man's arms dangled like a marionette.

Mikey laughed. "He looks like Howdy Doody."

Jax considered the man a moment. Arms flopping freely. "Yeah, he kinda does. Doesn't he?"

The man tried to speak.

"What's that?," said Jax. "Speak up. I can't hear you."

"I think his jaw is broken," said Mikey.

Jax smacked the man in the jaw. He let out a guttural cry.

"Yep. Broken," said Jax.

"Okay," said Mikey, "Finish up so we can get something to eat. I'm starving."

"Can we go to IHOP?" Jax asked.

"Sure. IHOP. Wherever. I just want to eat."

Mikey got cranky when he was hungry. Jax figured it was low blood sugar or something. He didn't want to listen to Mikey drone on about how hungry he was.

"Hold him," Jax said as he shoved the man into Mikey's arms.

Jax let loose with a flurry of rapid punches to the man's body. His fists a blur.

Mikey laughed as he held the man upright to take the beating Jax doled out.

Jax could have been a champion in the ring, Mikey thought. Maybe even one of those mixed martial arts fighters. Instead he unleashed all his rage and strength in back rooms and alleyways. Criminal. Lethal.

The man coughed. Wheezed. Then silence.

Jax landed another round of punches. Overkill.

"Give me a hand," Mikey said.

Jax grabbed the man's legs. Mikey held him under his limp and twisted arms. They hoisted the body and tossed it into a dumpster. Mikey closed the lid.

The two brothers took off latex gloves, balled them up, and threw them into a backpack. Mikey picked up the bag and slung it over his right shoulder.

Jax wiped his sweaty hands with a handkerchief. He folded the linen cloth and shoved it into his back pants pocket.

"IHOP?" said Jax.

"Yeah, little brother. Let's eat."

A cat mewed loudly and a metal trash can lid clanked on the pavement. The cat scurried into the shadows.

"Just an alley cat," said Jax.

"Better check. Just to be sure."

Jax nodded in agreement.

The two brothers did not like witnesses. And no witnesses ever came forward to testify against them. Hard for the dead to testify.

Jax and Mikey moved toward the trash cans.

"Run!" a young voice shouted from the darkness beyond the trash cans. Four shadowy figures sprinted out of the alley and disappeared around the corner.

Jax started after them when Mikey grabbed hold of his arm.

"Hold up. We'll never catch them."

Jax had lightning fast hands, but neither he nor Mikey could run worth a lick. They were big. Lumbering. But within reach, they were deadly.

"They probably saw everything," Jax said. "No loose ends. Ever."

"And there won't be."

Mikey tilted his head toward the ground. The glossy plastic from the front side of an ID card reflected in the lamplight. Mikey bent over and picked it up.

"One of them dropped this."

Mikey studied the card for a moment. "Looks fake. Says the guy is twenty-three."

He snorted. "My bet is eighteen or nineteen. Definitely not twenty-three."

"If it's a fake, how does that help us?" Jax said.

"Information is fake. The picture is real."

Mikey held the card up to Jax and pointed to the photo of the teenage male. "Somebody has seen this kid around here. Somebody knows his real name. We find that out and we find him. And his friends."

Jax smiled. "No loose ends."

"Never leave loose ends," Mikey said. They laughed as Mikey pocketed the ID card.

CHAPTER 2

DREW PATRICK

THE AROMA OF ARABICA beans rose with the steam from my cup of Dunkin' Donuts coffee. I was looking out my office window onto Brattle Street. The location just outside of Harvard Square made me feel smart.

A warm morning breeze drifted in through the open window. The calendar said September, but the weather still felt like August. I rubbed my eyes from staying up late to watch the conclusion of an extra innings Red Sox game. They beat the Yankees, so it was worth it. On to the playoffs.

The sidewalk below my office was crowded as students and professors made their way to morning classes. They jockeyed for sidewalk space with workers heading to occupy cubicles and offices throughout Cambridge and Boston.

A woman paused near the entrance to my building. She glanced at the sign out front.

HENDRICK'S & PEW, ATTORNEYS AT LAW
BRATTLE STREET PUBLISHING
ROBERT SAUNDERS, CPA
DREW PATRICK, PRIVATE INVESTIGATOR

The woman looked to be in her early forties and was dressed in a stylish business suit. Early morning meeting with her lawyer? A book agent pitching the next great American novel? In need of tax advice? She seemed too classy to be a potential client for me.

The woman stepped toward the building's front door. She wore sensible walking sneakers. A practical approach for walking and riding the T. She disappeared from my sight as she entered the building.

In the time it took for most people to reach the second floor and walk down the hallway there was a knock at my door. Dash lifted his head from his morning nap and looked in the direction of the knock.

I crossed my office and opened the door. The woman with the stylish business suit and sensible walking sneakers stood in front of me. Maybe I'm moving up in the world of private detecting.

"Mr. Patrick," she said. "My name is Bonnie Ross." She held out her right hand.

I took it and we shook. "Pleased to meet you, Ms. Ross. How may I help you?"

"Please, call me Bonnie. I'm worried about my daughter, and I'm hoping you can help."

"Please, come in."

I stepped aside to allow Bonnie Ross to enter my office.

Dash hopped down from his spot on the couch and walked over with his tail wagging.

"What kind of dog is he?" Bonnie asked.

"Beagle mix," I said.

"He's very handsome." She petted Dash on top of his head and scratched his big floppy ears. Friend for life. "What's his name?"

"Dash. But be careful about complimenting his looks, he already takes full advantage of his cuteness."

"I bet he does." Bonnie cracked a small smile. I liked her. A dog person and she thinks my jokes are funny.

"Have a seat," I said as I motioned to one of the chairs in front of my desk. "Would you like a cup of coffee? Tea? Water?"

"No. Thank you. Although the coffee smells heavenly."

"America runs on Dunkin," I said as I held up my coffee cup.

Bonnie offered another slight smile. She would have a warm, easy-going, smile if not troubled. People didn't usually hire a private investigator unless they were troubled about something.

Dash realized he was done getting attention and got back on the couch. He curled up, let out a sigh, and put his head down between his front paws. He whimpered.

"Ignore him," I said to Bonnie. "He has separation anxiety."

"But you're right here," Bonnie said.

"A work in progress."

I sat behind my desk. "Now, what can you tell me about the concern you have with your daughter?..." I left space at the end of my question.

"Tina," she said.

"What is your concern with Tina?"

"She is sixteen and a junior at Cambridge Rindge and Latin. She had always been a good student and had a nice group of friends. Never any trouble."

"Past tense?"

"Lately her grades have slipped. She's not failing," Bonnie paused a beat, "at least not yet. And she no longer spends time with her old friends."

"Does she seem depressed?" I asked. "Is she spending a lot of time alone?"

"No. At least I don't think so. Unless she is lying to me, Tina has been spending most of her time with a new group of friends. One of them is supposedly her boyfriend."

Bonnie stood and paced the floor. Dash raised his head. Hope springs eternal for a pat on the head or scratch behind the ear. When Bonnie didn't pay him any attention, Dash dropped his head back down and looked at me with his big brown eyes. Disappointed.

"Mr. Patrick," Bonnie said.

"Drew," I interjected.

Bonnie nodded and continued. "The truth is I don't know who these new friends are, where they are going, or what they are doing. Tina won't tell me anything. If I ground her, she just sneaks out."

"And you think they are a bad influence on Tina? Given the lower grades and lack of details about her new friends and activities?"

"Yes. And not knowing scares me." Tears began to roll down Bonnie's cheeks.

I handed her a box of tissues. She wiped her tears.

She seemed like a good mom dealing with a rebellious teen. Hopefully nothing serious with Tina's rebellion. Raising kids can be hard.

"And before you ask," she said, "there is no Mr. Ross in the picture. He took off when Tina was two. I haven't heard from him since."

I felt for Bonnie. I wanted to help. I just wasn't sure if there was much I could do beyond gathering information.

"As hard as I tried when I was a teenage boy, I'm no expert in teenage girls," I said. "Nonetheless, Private Investigator is printed on my business cards, so I can find out about Tina's new friends, where they go, and what they are doing."

Bonnie smiled through her tears. I was right. She had a warm and easy-going smile. Albeit with a hint of concern.

"That would be wonderful. At least I will have some information about that part of Tina's life she is keeping from me."

"Knowledge is power," I said.

"I only hope what we learn isn't as bad as some things I imagine," Bonnie said.

Bonnie didn't strike me as a worrier, but I was certain she could imagine some very bad things about Tina's secret life. She was a concerned single mother.

I had no experience as a parent, but I had dealt with many cases where a kid gets in trouble and things spiral out of control.

I thought about Ernest Hemingway writing in the *Sun Also Rises* where Mike went bankrupt "Gradually and then Suddenly." It could be like that for lots of things. Gradually kids start going down the wrong path, and then suddenly they are in a world of trouble.

CHAPTER 3

BONNIE ROSS GAVE ME the names of Tina's closest friends since childhood. While Tina hadn't been spending time with those friends in recent months, I figured it would still be worth talking to them. They were likely to know more than either Bonnie or I did at the moment. The four girls agreed to meet with me in the food court at CambridgeSide Galleria after school.

"Hello, handsome," said Jessica Casey when she answered her phone. "Are you calling with an offer to take me to lunch?"

"How about dinner? I'll even throw in an hour of shopping."

"Well, you love to eat. But you hate shopping. What's the catch?"

"Why does there have to be a catch?"

"Because we've already established you hate shopping."

Never try to argue with a lawyer. Well, former lawyer. Jessica left practicing law to become a private investigator with a fancy international private investigation firm headquartered in Boston.

"I have a case and need to speak with four teenage girls." I figured that explained it well enough.

"And you're afraid they have cooties?"

Jessica had a quick wit. And a sharp mind. They were two of the things I loved about her. Well, liked. Liked very much.

Perhaps bordering on love. Our Facebook status would be "It's complicated."

"Well, you never know," I said. "But mostly I don't want to seem creepy talking to four teenage girls in a mall. Not to mention they are more likely to open up to you."

"Because I'm a girl?"

"It can't hurt," I said. "And don't you often say what great private investigators women make because people are more comfortable talking to a female PI?"

"Casual empiricism would suggest that is true," she said.

"See, that is why you have the fancy office in Boston."

"Don't forget my expense account."

"That's right," I said. "Maybe you should buy dinner."

"Nice try," she said. "So, when and where are you meeting with these girls?"

"Food court at CambridgeSide Galleria. After school."

"Well, I could certainly go for a few hours of mall shopping, but you'll have to do better than the food court for dinner."

"I was thinking The Cheesecake Factory. But what's wrong with the food court?"

"I do love their cheesecake. And there is nothing wrong with the food court as fast food to fuel a day of marathon shopping. But a meal with your best gal deserves a proper sit down restaurant."

"I agree. Except for the marathon shopping part. And I do believe I offered one hour of shopping. Not a few hours."

"I thought that one slipped by you."

"I have a mind like a steel trap."

"So we're not negotiating?"

If we started negotiating on the shopping, I would lose. I knew it. Jessica knew it. We both knew it.

"I'm open to P.F. Chang's," I said. My best tactic.

"You can't blame a girl for trying." She let me off easy. It was probably because we hadn't seen each other in a few weeks due to her extensive travel for cases. There was also a good chance shopping would stretch beyond the original sixty minutes. *"I just need to try on one last pair of shoes,"* Jessica will say. The shoes always got me.

"So I'll see you at four?" I said.

"Not if I see you first."

We said goodbye and ended the call.

I sat at my computer to bang out final client reports for two insurance fraud cases I had just wrapped up. Between the reports, bathroom breaks for Dash, lunch, and a walk through Cambridge Common to stretch our legs, the day moved quickly. I hit send on an email and powered off the computer.

I steeled myself for an afternoon at the mall. I wasn't sure which I was dreading more – questioning four teenage girls or shopping. At least I would be with Jessica. Being with Jessica made both tasks tolerable.

"Want to go to doggy day camp?" I said to Dash.

His ears perked up, and he jumped off the couch. Dash rolled onto his back and began scratching it on the area rug. He approved of the plan. Or he had an itch. I couldn't tell which.

"Okay, let's go," I said. I grabbed Dash's leash off the hook by the door.

Dash flipped over and got onto his feet. His tail wagged at supersonic speed and his tongue hung out of his mouth.

Adventure awaited Dash at doggy day camp. Hours of play as he romped with his canine friends. It didn't get much better for Dash than running, climbing, and sniffing butts. Second only to lounging on the couch with his head in my lap. Maybe that was third on his list. Eating seemed to rule all.

I attached Dash's leash to his collar, and we were off.

CHAPTER 4

I TOOK MEMORIAL DRIVE. It was a mile longer than either Broadway or Cambridge Street, but I liked driving along the Charles River. The warmer weather encouraged outdoor activities as boats dotted the water and bikers peddled along the Dr. Paul Dudley White Bike Path.

I passed MIT on my left and could sense the brainpower solving complex problems. I continued further onto Edwin H. Land Boulevard, took a left on Binney Street, and a right onto First Street. I found a spot in the Galleria's parking garage and made my way to the food court.

I was a few minutes early, but I checked to see if either Jessica or the teens had arrived yet. I didn't spot Jessica. I pulled out my phone and glanced at the group picture Bonnie had texted me of Tina and her friends. Five young ladies smiling broadly. Absolutely giddy attending a Taylor Swift concert at Gillette Stadium. Happier times.

Not seeing the girls, I sat at an empty table overlooking Canal Park. I watched as tourists boarded a Charles River Boat for their seventy minute sightseeing tour along the Charles.

I received a text from Jessica. She was approaching the food court and wanted my location. I texted where I was sitting.

From across the food court I watched her approach. She had on one of those smart business suits like Bonnie had worn.

And all five feet and ten inches of her looked great in it. Jessica was both athletic and beautiful.

As she moved closer I noticed her shoulder length Chestnut hair swayed like in a shampoo commercial. I stood as she approached. We embraced and exchanged a quick kiss.

Jessica flashed a smile and sat down. She had a perfect smile. Actually, she was near perfect in every way. Everyone wondered why we hadn't more clearly defined our relationship. An excellent question without an easy answer.

"So, what do these girls look like?" said Jessica.

I handed her my phone with the picture.

"That was such a great concert," said Jessica.

I wrinkled my brow. "I didn't know you went to the Taylor Swift concert. I didn't even know you liked Taylor Swift."

"A little mystery keeps things interesting," said Jessica. "I brought Heather."

Heather was Jessica's niece. Twelve. Maybe thirteen now. I met her a few times. Sweet kid. No surprise she was a Taylor Swift fan. It seemed pretty much every tween and teen girl adored her.

"They should look pretty much the same," Jessica said handing my phone back to me. "The concert was only last year."

Jessica rested her hands atop the table and looked at me. "I'd like to go to Macy's first when we are done here." Her emerald eyes twinkled as she said it. Shopping always brought a twinkle to Jessica's eyes. Sometimes I did, too.

"I think you could easily burn your hour just in Macy's," I said. A gentle reminder of our agreement. My last best hope.

Jessica smiled at me again. "Do you remember when the Macy's was a Filene's?"

"I remember being in Filene's a time or two," I said.

"You once bought me a lovely sweater for Christmas from Filene's," said Jessica. "The burgundy cashmere one. I still have it."

Jessica thought for a moment. "Filene's had been around for a long time," she said. "Over a hundred years."

"And Lechmere," I said. "Where the Best Buy is now. The original Lechmere store and Green Line station both got their names from being located in Lechmere Square."

"Well," Jessica said, "you're a regular Cliff Clavin."

"Just sharing a little piece of local history."

Both Filene's and Lechmere had gone bankrupt in the increasingly competitive retail landscape. I wondered if, like Mike in *The Sun Also Rises*, bankruptcy comes slowly and then suddenly for department stores? My train of thought was broken as I heard Jessica's voice.

"When the girls arrive, try not to be intimidating."

"While I admit I can do intimidating extremely well when called upon," I said, "I don't think my mere presence as intimidating."

"It can be."

"How am I being intimidating at the moment?"

"Sitting you're fine," she said. "But standing you can cast an imposing shadow."

"It's not like I'm Andre the Giant."

"Drew, you're six foot two and athletic."

"Tom Brady's six foot four and athletic," I said. "I doubt the girls would find him intimidating or casting an imposing shadow."

Jessica looked at me with a smirk on her face. "Really? You're comparing them meeting you to meeting Tom Brady?"

"What? It's a valid point."

"Drew, honey, you are very handsome. I don't have eyes for anyone else –"

I held up my hand to stop her. "No need to say any more," I said. "I'm not sure my bruised ego could take it."

Jessica kissed me on the cheek. She said, "Have I ever told you what I thought the first time we met?"

"Yes. But I wouldn't mind hearing it again."

"I took a look at your wavy dark hair, piercing blue eyes, and dimpled chin and thought, *wow*! There is a handsome looking man."

"And then I swept you off your feet with my charm, intelligence, and overall toughness."

"Something like that," she said.

"There they are," I said with a tilt of my head toward the Au Bon Pain.

The four teens looked at me, glanced at their phones, and back to me. One of them said something. The other three nodded. They started walking toward our table.

CHAPTER 5

JESSICA STOOD AS THEY approached. Given our recent conversation, I wondered if I should remain seated. I thought I might appear rude. I stood, being careful to keep my intimidation and imposing shadow in check.

"I'm Drew, and this is Jessica," I said.

Four pairs of eyes looked us each over for a beat. They seemed neither intimidated by me nor like they were standing in an imposing shadow. Good for the present situation, but I'd need to practice later to make sure I wasn't going soft.

"I'm Madison. This is Olivia, Savannah, and Haley."

Madison wore the same Taylor Swift concert shirt as in the picture. Olivia wore a PINK shirt. I wasn't sure if that was the pop singer or Victoria's Secret line of clothing. Savannah and Haley wore shirts from either Old Navy or the Gap. I wasn't sure about that either. All four wore skinny jeans.

"You look older in person," Savannah said to me.

Brutal honesty.

"The picture on my website is a few years old," I said. "But like wine, I get better with age."

No reaction. Clearly not my crowd.

"Where did you sit for the concert?" Jessica said to Madison as she considered the Taylor Swift shirt.

Yep. That's Jessica. Saving my bacon right out of the gate. I at least deserve some credit for having the foresight to invite her along.

"Like around the fifty yard line," said Madison. "Pretty awesome seats."

The other girls nodded their heads in agreement.

"Best. Show. Ever." said Olivia.

"And there was that cute guy who was hitting on you," Savannah said to Olivia.

"He was soooo cute," said Haley. "He totally wanted you."

"Sounds like it was a fun evening," I said. "But we don't want to take up too much of your time."

The four teens looked at me. Buzz kill.

"Thank you for meeting with us," said Jessica.

"Whatever," said Madison. Her attitude cooled now that we were no longer talking about Taylor Swift or cute boys.

"Please, have a seat," I said.

The girls each took a seat around the table. Jessica and I sat back in our chairs.

"So you're a real private detective?" said Savannah.

Perhaps a thaw was underway.

"Yes," I said. "We both are. Jessica works for a large investigation firm in Boston. I am self-employed."

"So you couldn't get a job at Jessica's company?" said Haley.

So much for the thaw. My credentials being questioned by a sixteen-year-old high school junior.

"Drew could work anywhere," said Jessica. "He chooses to work for himself. In fact, he was once an agent with the FBI."

"Why did you leave the FBI?" Olivia said.

How did this become about me?

"Were you fired?" said Madison.

Now they were tag-teaming me.

"Or did you just wash out?" said Savannah.

Everybody get in on the action. Pile on.

"Neither," I said. "I decided I wanted a change."

"Mid-life crisis?" said Madison.

"How old do you think I am?" I said. "Never mind. I'm not sure I want to know."

"What can you tell us about Tina?" said Jessica to the rescue, again.

Jessica gave me her *you're welcome* glance. I was at the ready to meet her with my *thank you* glance.

"What do you want to know?" said Olivia.

"When was the last time you saw her?" I said.

"We see her in school," said Savannah.

"Yeah. Just saw her a few hours ago," added Haley.

"What about outside of school?" said Jessica.

The girls were silent a beat. They glanced at each other. Sad eyes.

"You don't hang out with Tina outside of school any longer?" I said.

"No," said Madison. "Not really." There was disappointment in her voice.

"She ditched us for Aaron and his friends," said Olivia.

"Is Aaron her boyfriend?" said Jessica.

"She says he is," said Savannah. "Never met him. Don't know for sure."

"He went to a different school than us," said Haley. "Plus he graduated last year."

"Is he in college locally?" I asked. "Have a job someplace?" Master detective at work.

The four teens shrugged their shoulders. The universal *don't know*.

"Aaron's bad news," said Savannah. Disdain in her voice.

"How so?" I said.

"He drinks," said Olivia. "And smokes weed."

"What about Tina? She drinking? Smoking weed?" said Jessica.

A few beats passed. No one answered. The four teens looked at each other.

"We're not trying to get Tina in trouble," I said. "The exact opposite. If she's in any kind of trouble, we want to help."

"Even if she doesn't hang out with us much any more, Tina's still our friend," said Haley.

They wanted to be loyal. I got that. I could also tell they were concerned.

"We don't like her being with Aaron. Or the others," said Madison.

"She's different now," said Savannah.

"Because she's drinking? Getting high?" I said.

The four teens nodded their heads sheepishly.

"Do you know Aaron's last name? Where he lives?" said Jessica.

"Hurley," said Olivia. "Aaron Hurley. Not sure where he lives."

"What about Aaron's friends?" I said. "Do you know who they are?"

"Not really," said Madison. "Their names are Carla and Stewart. That's all we know."

"Do you have any pictures?" I asked.

"Tina sent us a selfie with Aaron when they first started dating," said Madison. "Wanted to show him off. We don't have any pictures with Stewart and Carla."

"Can you send me the picture of Tina and Aaron?" I said.

Madison nodded and then her fingers moved across the screen of her phone. My phone dinged with a new text message. I looked at the attached photo. A selfie of Tina and Aaron on a Swan Boats ride in the Boston Public Garden. They appeared normal teens. On a normal date.

"What about Tina's social media?" I said. "Any clues there? I checked Facebook and couldn't find anything."

The girls looked at me like I was an idiot. At best that I was clueless. I wasn't exactly on a roll with them.

"Facebook is for old people," said Savannah. "You know," she paused a beat, "like you."

Savannah strikes again. What age did she consider old? Whatever it was, I had passed it.

"Tina was on Instagram and Snapchat," said Madison. "She doesn't really use her accounts anymore."

"Could she have new accounts you don't know about?" Jessica said.

"Maybe," said Haley.

"Anything else you can think about?" I said.

"Talk to a guy named Bobby," said Savannah. "I don't know his last name. Tina mentioned a Bobby hooked them up with fake IDs. He works at some club called the Snake something."

"The Snake Pit?" I said.

"Yeah. That's it," said Savannah.

She seemed somewhat impressed I came up with the name. Score one for the old guy.

Except the Snake Pit was bad news on many levels. So much for two normal teens going on normal dates. But the drinking and weed had been bad signs already. The Snake Pit just made things worse.

But I had new information. Leads to follow-up on. In detective land that is progress.

"Thank you all," I said, "you've been a big help."

"Can you really help Tina?" said Madison. Her voice layered in concern.

"I'm going to do my best," I said.

I didn't know whether they thought my best was good enough.

The more I thought about it, the more troubled I was with what we had learned. The Snake Pit was no place for a teenage girl to be going. It was no place for any decent human being to be going. Breaking news that day was a beaten body found in a dumpster in the alley behind the Snake Pit. Not the first time for that dumpster. Likely not the last.

The girls showed no awareness of the news, so I didn't bring it up. No need to worry them about Tina anymore than they already were. Maybe they wouldn't find out. Most teens aren't news wonks.

The girls left and did whatever teenage girls do in a shopping mall. Jessica got a start at Macy's while I called Bonnie with an update.

Unlike our four teens, Bonnie had seen the news. Like any good parent would, she freaked when I mentioned the Snake Pit as part of the narrative. Yes, it was horrible. Yes, the Snake

Pit was no place for her daughter to be going. But I did my level best to let Bonnie know it was unlikely the two had anything to do with each other. We agreed to set it aside. At least for the moment.

Bonnie still wanted to confront Tina that evening and ask her if it were all true. Fake ID. Drinking. Weed. Going to the Snake Pit.

Her plan was to ground Tina. Confiscate her fake ID. Forbid Tina from seeing Aaron. Prevent her from going to the Snake Pit.

All reasonable. All things most parents would do in the same situation. All made perfect sense to me. Nonetheless, I asked her to wait.

First, I wasn't convinced Tina would obey. She might run. And Tina on the run complicated matters. Second, I hadn't even put in the time to cover Bonnie's initial payment for my minimum one day of detecting. I owed her what she already paid for.

Related to point number two was the fact I hadn't completed a thorough enough investigation. As much as Tina's former BFFs were helpful, I needed to confirm what Madison, Olivia, Savannah, and Haley told me. I should speak with Bobby and, most importantly, with Aaron. At that point I could more confidently close the case and submit my final report to Bonnie.

Bonnie said she and Tina were having dinner with Bonnie's parents, so Tina would be with her for the evening. No Aaron. No Snake Pit. As hard as it would be, Bonnie would hold off. I told her that I should know more the next day and I would contact her when I did.

After we hung up I let out a sigh. I had been honest with Bonnie with what I knew. I owed her that. What I didn't reveal was my sense of concern.

I hoped all my detecting would do was confirm information we currently had. It was bad enough. But could be dealt with. I would file my report, offer resources to assist Bonnie and Tina, be there if needed to help. Otherwise, case closed for Drew Patrick, Private Investigator.

What I feared was there being more to the story. There almost always was in cases like Tina's. The Snake Pit was an easy place to get into trouble. The kind of trouble Bonnie had been dreading. Maybe even worse.

CHAPTER 6

JAX AND MIKEY

"LET US HELP YOU WITH those Mrs. O'Donnell," Mikey said.

Jax and Mikey each took a grocery bag out of their elderly neighbor's trunk.

"Such nice boys. Thank you," Mrs. O'Donnell said.

They ascended the stairs of the three-story walk-up. Mrs. O'Donnell lived in the apartment on the second floor. Jax and Mikey lived in the apartment on the third.

"I remember when you two barely came up to my knee," said Mrs. O'Donnell. Jax and Mikey grew up here. They had been neighbors with Mrs. O'Donnell their entire lives.

"Let me get my keys out," said Mrs. O'Donnell as she dug through her purse.

"Take your time, Mrs. O'Donnell," said Jax.

"Here they are."

Mrs. O'Donnell turned the key in the lock and opened her door.

"You boys go ahead."

Jax and Mikey entered Mrs. O'Donnell's apartment and put the grocery bags on her kitchen table.

"Do you want help to put your groceries away?" Mikey said.

"No, I'll be fine. Thank you."

Mrs. O'Donnell pulled two dollar bills out of her purse. "Here you go," she said handing a dollar each to Jax and Mikey. Mrs. O'Donnell tried to pay them whenever they helped her carrying in groceries, taking out trash, or shoveling out her car in the winter. The two brothers always politely refused to take even a penny.

"No, Ma'am," Mikey said.

"Yeah, it is our pleasure," Jax said.

"Such nice boys."

"Have a good day, Mrs. O'Donnell," said Mikey as he and Jax left her apartment.

"Say hello to your mother for me."

"We will," Jax said.

"Sweet old lady," Mikey said once they were in the hallway.

"Yeah."

Jax and Mikey climbed the next flight of stairs to the third floor. As little boys they would slide down the railing.

"Ma, we're home," Mikey called out as the two entered the apartment.

It wasn't much. A simple two bedroom and one bath unit. And it hadn't changed in thirty years. Same wallpaper, furniture, and decorations. Old school portraits of Jax and Mikey covered one living room wall.

Gwen Crane came out of the kitchen. She moved slowly and was gaunt. Her hair matted from sleeping. She gave each of her boys a kiss on the cheek.

"Mrs. O'Donnell says hello," Mikey said.

"That's sweet," Gwen said.

"How you feeling today, Ma?" Jax said.

"Fine. Just fine. How was work?"

"Good," Mikey answered. "Busy."

"I wish you boys could find a job with regular hours."

"We like our job."

"And the pay is good," added Jax.

Jax and Mikey told their mother they worked security at a downtown Boston office building. Mostly the late shift. She had no idea what her boys actually did. Or how violently they carried out their work. If she ever found out, it would crush her.

"Can I fix you something to eat?" she said.

"We ate at IHOP," Jax replied.

"I know how much you love their pancakes," she said, pinching Jax's cheeks. Gwen moved between her two boys and sat on the sofa.

"We just came home to check on you," Mikey said. "We picked up an extra job today. A little security gig on the side."

Total lie. A lie Mikey justified to protect their mother.

"It's not that I don't appreciate all you boys do. You keep this roof over our heads, food on the table, and pay . . ." her words were interrupted with a coughing fit. The emphysema was getting worse.

"Get her something drink," Mikey said as he elbowed Jax.

Jax went into the kitchen and returned with a glass of water. "Here you go, Ma."

She took the glass and drank. When Gwen finished, she placed it on the coffee table in front her.

"Thank you, sweetie. Now, as I was saying -"

"Ma, it's okay," Mikey said.

"Don't interrupt your mother."

"Yes, Ma'am. Sorry, Ma."

"Now, I appreciate all you boys do. I know my medical bills are high."

Jax opened his mouth to speak and then shut it when his mother held up her hand.

"You two boys have been such a blessing to me. Since the day you were born. Never thought I would have twin boys."

Gwen shook her head. "No, never thought I'd have twins. But look at you two. So strong and handsome."

Mikey rolled his eyes with a slight shake of his head. He was glad he and Jax were fraternal and not identical twins. Jax had a face only their mother could love.

"And you take such good care of me," she continued. "I do wish you would find yourselves some nice young ladies and settle down. Get married. Give me grandchildren."

"One day, Ma," Mikey said.

"I've heard that before," she said.

Gwen pushed herself up from the couch. Jax and Mikey helped her to her feet.

"I'm going to take a nap."

"Let us know if you need anything," Mikey said.

"I need grandchildren," said Gwen as she shuffled down the short hallway to her bedroom. After she closed her bedroom door, Jax and Mikey went into the kitchen. Mikey opened the fridge and pulled out two beers. He handed one to Jax.

"She isn't ever going to give up on the grand kids thing," Jax said as he opened his beer.

"Don't think so." Mikey opened his beer and took a tug on the bottle.

Jax leaned against the counter. "So, what's the plan?"

"We talk to Bobby. If he doesn't know who the kid is, he can tell us who does."

"What if those kids talk? You know, tell their parents? Or go to the cops?"

"They haven't yet. News is already reporting about the body being found in the dumpster. No witnesses have come forward. No one knows nothing."

"What if the cops offer a reward for information? Maybe the kids will talk then."

"Maybe, but what are they going to say? We were in a dark alley. Hard to make a positive ID."

"But we can't take any chances. Right?"

"Never," Mikey said. "Don't worry little bro, we'll find them and make certain they never tell another living soul what they saw."

"You're only one minute older than me," Jax said.

"Still makes me your big brother."

Mikey mussed Jax's hair.

"Stop. I hate when you do that."

Mikey did it again. Jax grabbed him and they started wrestling.

"What's going out there?!" Gwen yelled from her bedroom.

"Sorry, Ma!" Mikey said.

"Yeah, sorry, Ma!"

Mikey took a final sip of his beer and placed the bottle in the sink. "Come on, let's go talk to Bobby."

"I haven't finished my beer."

"Finish it on the way."

"We're not supposed to have open containers in the car."

Mikey gave Jax his *are you kidding me?* Stare.

"Don't worry, I'm driving," Mikey said.

"I'd feel better if I just finished my beer first."

"Fine, you big baby. Finish your beer. Then we'll go talk to Bobby."

Jax chugged the half bottle of beer. He wiped his mouth and burped.

"You're disgusting."

Jax's mouth formed a crooked smile. Mikey knew the look. Jax was thinking about going to town on Bobby.

"Slow your roll," Mikey said. "I have something else in mind."

Disappointment showed on Jax's face.

"Don't pout," said Mikey. "It will still be fun."

"You promise?" said Jax.

"Yeah, little bro. I promise. Your backpack still in the car?"

"On the backseat."

"Good. We need to make a little stop to fill it."

The two brothers exited the apartment.

Time to get back to work.

CHAPTER 7

BOBBY LIVED IN A RUNDOWN place at the edge of one of Boston's sketchier neighborhoods. Redevelopment and gentrification stalled with the Great Recession in 2008. When the economy improved, everyone forgot the grand plans they had for this little corner of Beantown.

It suited Bobby just fine. He had been forced out of neighborhoods with increasing rents before. He liked his place. Rent was cheap. No one bothered him. He liked to be left alone.

To say Bobby was not happy to see Jax and Mikey show up at his door would be the understatement of the year. Besides valuing his privacy, Bobby knew Jax and Mikey from the Snake Pit. Nobody from the Snake Pit wanted Jax and Mikey standing at their front door.

"You going to invite us in?" Mikey said to Bobby.

Before Bobby had a chance to speak, Jax and Mikey pushed their way past him into the tiny studio apartment.

"You live alone?" Jax said as he looked around.

"Yeah," Bobby said. "Rent's cheap."

"Looks like it would be," Mikey replied.

"What can I do for you gentlemen?"

"Gentlemen?" Mikey said. "You hear that, Jax?"

"Yeah, Mikey. Pretty funny."

Jax and Mikey howled with laughter.

"We're not gentlemen," Mikey said. "Except with ladies. Women deserve our respect."

Bobby stood in stunned silence. He did not want to piss these two off by saying the wrong thing.

"What's the matter?" Jax said. "Cat got your tongue?"

"N..N..No."

"You got a stuttering problem?" Mikey said.

"No. Sorry. Just nervous, I guess."

"What are you nervous about?" Mikey said. "Just some friends stopping by for a chat."

Bobby nodded timidly. "You want something to drink?"

"No. We won't be here long," Mikey said. He reached into his jacket pocket.

Bobby flinched.

"Twitchy little fella," Jax noted.

"We can appear a little intimidating," Mikey said. "Relax, Bobby. I just want to show you this." Mikey handed the fake ID from the alley to Bobby.

Bobby studied it a moment.

"Do you know the kid?"

Bobby considered the picture on the ID a moment longer. He then nodded his head.

"Yeah. I know him."

"Name?" Mikey said. "Other than the phony one printed on that card?"

"Aaron. Aaron Hurley."

"You hear that, Jax. Aaron Hurley."

"Aaron Hurley," Jax repeated.

Mikey took Aaron's fake ID back from Bobby and pocketed it.

"What can you tell us about Mr. Aaron Hurley?" Mikey said.

"What do you want to know?" Bobby wanted to be as helpful as possible. Aaron was definitely in deep shit if Jax and Mikey were asking about him. But he had his own skin to save.

"Do you know where he lives?"

"I think he still lives with his parents in Chestnut Hill. I can give you the address. Went over there a few times in high school."

Mikey thought about how far down Bobby had fallen from growing up in Chestnut Hill. Being a junkie has a way of doing that to a person.

"That would be very helpful," said Mikey. "What can you tell us about his friends?"

"Friends?" said Bobby as he hunted for pen and paper.

"Who are the other kids Aaron hangs out with at the Snake Pit?" Mikey said.

"I don't know them. I mean I've seen them with Aaron, but I've never really talked to them. I can tell you the names on their IDs, but they're fakes. You know, like Aaron's."

Bobby located a discarded utility bill envelope. He continued looking for a pen. Mikey pulled a pen from his pocket and handed it to Bobby.

"Thanks," Bobby said as he took the pen from Mikey. He wrote down Aaron's address in Chestnut Hill and handed the envelope to Mikey.

"Don't forget the pen," Mikey said. "It was a gift."

Considering it a gift was Mikey's way of saying he had lifted from the body of a CEO who couldn't pay his debt.

"It's a real nice pen," Bobby said as he handed it back to Mikey.

"A Montblanc," Jax noted.

Mikey folded the envelope and put it in his pocket along with the Montblanc.

"You've been very helpful, Bobby," Mikey said.

"Aim to please." Bobby was relieved Jax and Mikey would be leaving happy.

"We're almost done here," Mikey said.

Jax took the backpack off his shoulder. He opened it and pulled out a new pair of latex gloves.

Bobby's eyes looked at Jax quizzically. They shifted to Mikey as Jax tossed the backpack over to his brother.

"What's going on, guys?" Bobby said, his voice trembling.

Jax slipped the gloves on and then grabbed Bobby. He forced him onto the mattress in the corner. Bobby watched Mikey also pull on a similar pair of gloves.

"Don't worry, Bobby. The high will be amazing," Mikey said.

He prepared a needle and syringe for injection. Mikey stepped toward Bobby. Jax had him pinned to the mattress.

"Hold on, fellas," said Bobby. He tried to break free. Not a chance.

"Bobby you've been a tremendous help," said Bobby. "But we can't take the chance you might tell someone we inquired about Aaron Hurley."

"Like the cops," said Jax.

Mikey looked at Jax sideways.

"I won't tell. Honest. Please, you don't have to do this."

"But we do," Mikey said. "Like I was saying, you knowing about our interest in Aaron Hurley is a loose end for us. We can't have loose ends."

"What did Aaron do? If he owes you money, he'll pay up. I'll see that he does."

"He saw something," Mikey said. "He and his friends. Something they shouldn't have."

"Aaron won't talk," Bobby said. "None of them will talk."

"You're probably right about that, but we can't take the chance. You see, they're also loose ends."

"We don't like loose ends," Jax added.

"Please," pleaded Bobby, "let me talk to them. I'll take care of everything. I swear."

"We're done talking," Mikey said.

"Please!" Bobby was crying.

Mikey rolled up Bobby's sleeve and tied a band around his arm. He looked for the perfect spot. The old track marks made it easy.

"No! Please, no!" Bobby screamed.

Jax and Mikey ignored him. Mikey plunged the needle into Bobby's arm. There was enough heroin to kill a man Jax's size. Bobby was much smaller.

They waited until Bobby was still. Jax let go. Mikey made sure to get Bobby's fingerprints on the syringe. He dropped it onto the mattress next to Bobby's hand.

"So sad when a junkie has a relapse," Mikey said.

"Truly sad," Jax said.

The two brothers laughed as they took off their latex gloves and put them in the backpack.

They exited Bobby's apartment.

Time to a pay a visit to Aaron Hurley in Chestnut Hill.

CHAPTER 8

DREW PATRICK

AFTER ENDURING TWO hours of shopping and then a pleasant dinner with Jessica, I headed to the Snake Pit to speak with Bobby.

I was hoping he would give me Aaron's address. Speaking with Aaron apart from Tina would tell me a lot. Bobby and Aaron had been high school classmates, so at the very least I should get the town. Bobby might also prove helpful in giving me more insight into Aaron Hurley. Good to know more about how a person thinks and might behave.

I found a well-lit spot in the Snake Pit's parking lot and parked my car. I'm not sure the lamplight mattered all that much in preventing a break-in, but I figured it wouldn't hurt. I thought about bringing Dash to ward off potential thieves, but it was a coin toss whether he would give them a sloppy wet kiss or bark at them. I tended to lean more toward the sloppy wet kiss. My parents would be spoiling their granddog for the evening.

A quick call to my mother and she was more than happy to pick Dash up from doggy day camp and dog sit. It saved my boarding him for the evening. Not that Dash minded spending the night in one of the dog suites, but I knew he would prefer an evening at my parents.

There was already a line forming to get into the Snake Pit. I walked past it to the bouncer at the front door. Paint him green and he would resemble the Incredible Hulk. I showed him my PI license and asked to speak with Bobby.

"Bobby aint here," Hulk said.

"He off tonight?" I asked.

"Bobby's dead," he said without emotion.

"Dead? When did that happen?"

"Earlier today. Drug overdose."

Learning Bobby was dead from an overdose should have been a shock, but it wasn't. Sadly, it wasn't that uncommon for anyone associated with the Snake Pit. Except maybe Hulk. He looked like a health nut.

"Anyone else I can talk to?" I said.

"Pete's the manager."

"May I speak with Pete?"

"Pete," Hulk said into a wire, "got a PI out here wants to talk to you about Bobby." He paused a beat as Pete said something.

"Looks like the real deal," Hulk said as he glanced my way. "License seemed legit." He paused another beat to listen to Pete again. "Okay."

Hulk opened the front door and nodded me in. "Pete's at the bar."

"Thanks," I said.

I stepped through the front door. The Snake Pit had black walls with a variety of snakes painted on them. I would have gone for a different theme.

Employees hurried about getting ready for the club to open for the night. Through the dim lighting, I could see two guys talking at the bar. My keen detective skills led me to believe the guy behind the bar was the bartender. The other guy must be Pete.

I walked over and introduced myself. The bartender moved away. The guy standing at the bar looked at me.

"I'm Pete," he said. Nailed it. Drew Patrick, master sleuth.

"Thanks for taking a moment to speak with me," I said. Win them over with kindness.

"A quick moment," said Pete. "We're about to open for the evening. Although I don't know what I can tell you. Cops came by asking about Bobby. Said he died of an overdose at home. Ruled accidental."

"I'm sorry to hear about Bobby."

"A damn shame," said Pete. "Bobby had been clean for a year." Pete shook his head.

"Working here probably didn't help with his twelve-step program," I said.

Pete didn't react to my comment. But he knew what went on at his club.

"What was Bobby's full name?" I asked. I wasn't sure his death was relevant to my investigation, but I figured it was better to have it, than not.

"Sampson. Bobby Sampson. Robert, if we're going by his official employee file."

"Thanks." I wrote the name in my notepad.

"I actually came to ask Bobby about an Aaron Hurley," I said.

"Don't know that name."

I showed Pete the picture of Tina and Aaron.

"I've seen those two in here. Is the guy Aaron Hurley?"

"Yeah. The girl is Tina Ross. Both underage."

"Hey, man. We don't knowingly serve anyone under twenty-one."

"You should probably step up your screening for fake IDs," I suggested.

Pete nodded, but didn't elaborate on his plan. If he even had one. I doubted he did. Not at a place like the Snake Pit.

"Aaron and Tina come in often?" I said.

"Couple times a week. Another guy and girl are usually with them."

Stewart and Carla.

"Underage as well," I said. Just to make the point. No reaction from Pete.

"When were they here last you can remember?" I asked.

Pete thought for a moment. "They were here last night."

"Same night that guy got beat to death, and the body tossed in your dumpster?"

Pete said, "As it happens. You don't think they were involved?"

"No. Just trying to establish facts. Did they interact with the deceased before his demise?"

"Not that I know of."

Hard to see a connection between Tina's group and the dead guy. Nonetheless, due diligence never hurt an investigation. Go where the conversation leads.

"I'm sure you went over this with the police investigating the murder, but do you know who the guy interacted with? The police express interest in anyone? Someone who could be a suspect?"

"No." A one-word answer. Direct. Short and not so sweet. Pete didn't like the question. He was probably sick of being asked about patrons at his club ending up dead in the alley.

I nodded. No point in pressing on that issue. Again, probably unrelated to Tina and company. I returned to my original line of questioning.

"Did Bobby work last night?"

"Yeah. He's here . . ." Pete paused a beat. "Bobby worked every night." A hint of sadness in his voice. Even people in notorious clubs, located in sketchy neighborhoods, have people they care about.

"Do you know if Bobby and Aaron spoke last night?" I said.

Pete shrugged. "Don't know." A two-word answer. No less irritated with the question. Maybe Pete just didn't like me. Or he was sick of answering questions in general. I'm a pretty charming guy. Must be the questioning Pete doesn't like.

"They knew each other from high school," I told Pete. "According to some of Tina's other friends, Bobby hooked them up with the fake IDs."

This didn't appear to surprise Pete. Which didn't surprise me. Tried as I might, Pete was getting harder to like.

"Any interaction between Bobby and the guy who ended up in the dumpster?" A more likely scenario than Tina and her friends. Maybe no more relevant. But I like being thorough.

"I don't know," Pete said. "This is a busy place. I can't possibly know every conversation going on."

"I don't expect you would," I said. "Again, I'm just trying to gather as many facts as I can."

Loud music thumped through the club speakers. Purple strobe lights flashed. We were moments from opening time. A good time to leave. I felt I had gotten all I was going to get out of Pete.

"Thanks for your time," I said to Pete. "Call me if you think of anything else." I handed him my business card.

Pete took my card and stuck it in his shirt pocket. I doubted Pete would call if he did think of anything else. He might just use my card as kindling to light a joint.

I exited the Snake Pit just before the crowd began spilling through the front door.

Talking to people didn't always advance investigations. Pete didn't offer much. I could confirm Tina, Aaron, Stewart, and Carla frequent the Snake Pit. I also confirmed Aaron knew Bobby.

What I had learned was that Bobby was dead from an overdose. I also learned Tina, Aaron, Stewart, and Carla happened to be at the Snake Pit last night when a man's body was left in the dumpster behind the club.

I couldn't see how the last two were connected. Most likely a coincidence. But as a general rule, I don't like coincidences. At least not ones I can't explain. I needed to know more than I did. I needed to speak with Aaron Hurley.

CHAPTER 9

I TOOK A BITE OF MY bacon, egg, and cheese sandwich. Crumbs from the croissant flaked onto my desk. Dash sat at my feet with eagle eyes fixed on every bite I took.

"If you're good, I'll give you a piece when I'm done," I told him. His floppy ears perked up, and he tilted his head. I'm not sure how many words he recognized, but I knew he understood the general gist of what I was saying. We had played a similar scene out many mornings.

I followed another bite of the sandwich with a sip of coffee. The two-handed breakfast. Sandwich in one hand. Coffee in the other. Efficient. Time saving.

Not fast enough for Dash. He whimpered and nudged my leg with his snout.

"In a minute," I said.

I took a few more bites, followed by another sip of coffee. I left a respectable piece of sandwich for Dash. I handed it to him. He inhaled it. I think he liked the Cherrywood Smoked bacon part the best. Hard to tell. It was gone so fast.

"That's it. All gone."

Dash checked the floor to make sure nothing was missed. When he was satisfied all was clear and another sandwich wouldn't appear, he trotted over the couch and hopped up. He circled once and plopped down on the Red Sox blanket in his corner of the couch. He let out a sigh and put down his head. A few minutes later he was snoring. What a life.

I turned to my computer. A quick Internet search told me there are over five thousand Hurley's in Massachusetts. Nearly four thousand of them lived in the greater Boston area. Even filtering by Aaron Hurley and age didn't narrow the list down enough to be practical. Likely an unlisted address and phone number for Aaron's parents. Aaron probably just had a cell phone.

I called a guy I know at the DMV and left a message. He didn't owe me any favors, so I would have to barter. The last DMV record search cost me two Patriots tickets. Fifty yard line, no less. Those set me back a hefty portion of one of my more lucrative cases.

While I had contacts with the police, and several close friends still in the FBI, I didn't like to cash in those chips unless necessary. There were always more questions involved. And then I needed to keep law enforcement in the loop. I wasn't at a point in my investigation where I was prepared to take on the additional responsibility.

I tipped back in my chair and stared at the ceiling. I do some of my best thinking staring at my office ceiling.

I had no great revelation. I didn't magically conjure up Aaron Hurley's address.

My cell phone rang. I tipped forward in my chair and reached for my phone. My contact at the DMV returning my call.

"Cosmo, thanks for calling me back."

"I told you not to use my name."

Cosmo is a bit of conspiracy theorist. And when I say a bit of a conspiracy theorist, I mean he's a pretty far gone conspiracy theorist.

Caution is taken in sending and receiving messages. Usually in code. Using a system of his own creation.

A bit of a pain, but Cosmo's information is useful. Both for his access to DMV records, and his other contacts.

"Right. Sorry," I said. "Any luck?"

"Yes, I'll send it to you the usual way."

"I'll be waiting."

"Now," Cosmo said, "for the matter of payment."

"Of course. What's your price?"

"Billy Joel is playing at Fenway Park. The best seats you can get. And not the best you say you can get. The actual best you can get."

"I'm on it," I said. "I didn't know you were a fan."

"He's the Piano Man. It's a concert at Fenway. Magical combination."

I told Cosmo I'd deliver the tickets to him and we ended our call. I made a note to contact my friend in the concert promotion business. He owed me a favor for a case I worked pro bono a few months back.

I checked my email for the coded message Cosmo sent. I opened my desk drawer and pulled out the decipher notebook Cosmo had given me. I grabbed my notepad and a pen and began decoding. After a few minutes I knew Aaron Hurley was eighteen years-old and where he lived in Chestnut Hill.

"Want to go for a ride?" I said to Dash.

He woke and jumped off the couch. I attached his leash.

"Okay, let's go."

Dash and I walked downstairs and exited onto Brattle Street. Dash peed on a bush next to the entrance to the building. We walked a block to the small parking lot where I rented a parking space. We got in my car and I pointed it toward Chestnut Hill.

After the first five minutes of the twenty-minute ride Dash lost interest in looking out the window. He curled up and took a nap. He sat back up when we turned into Aaron's neighborhood. He whined at being in unfamiliar territory. Anxiety. A work in process.

I pulled in front of the address Cosmo gave me. I parked under a large tree for shade. Aaron's parents had done well for themselves. The Hurley's lived in one of the largest and most opulent houses on a street of large and opulent houses.

I cracked the windows for fresh air. In the shade it was cool.

"I'll be right back," I told Dash as I got out of the car.

He whined as I walked toward the house. He settled down when he realized he could still see me at the front door.

I rang the doorbell. I waited a few beats. All was quiet. I rang the doorbell again. I waited another minute, then the front door opened. Aaron Hurley stood facing me.

"Can I help you?" Aaron said. He wore a swimsuit and Boston College tee shirt.

"My name is Drew Patrick. I'm a private investigator."

I handed Aaron one of my cards. He took it and considered it a moment. He seemed unimpressed. I thought it was a nice looking card. Designed it myself.

"I've been hired by Tina's mom."

"So. What's that got to do me with me?"

"You and Tina are dating?"

"Do I need a lawyer or something?"

"I'm not the police."

"Then I don't really need to talk to you." Aaron began closing the door. I stuck my foot out and stopped the door from closing.

"No. You don't need to speak with me. But I'd appreciate it if you did. Just a few minutes of your time."

Aaron rolled his eyes. "Whatever, Dude. Just make it fast." He pulled the door back open.

"I'm not here to get you into trouble. Frankly, what you do is none of my concern. But Tina's mom hired me to look into Tina's activities."

"And?"

"Tina's activities include you. So I need to know what Tina is up to."

"Tina's a big girl. She doesn't need her mommy looking out for her. She certainly doesn't need a rent a cop snooping around."

"Private Investigator."

"Huh?"

"I'm a private investigator. Licensed by the Commonwealth of Massachusetts."

Aaron waved his hands and wagged his head. "Touchy," he said.

"Just clarifying. Facts matter."

Another eye roll from Aaron. I figured I should get right to the point before I completely lost his attention.

"Look," I said, "Tina is sixteen. Which means she's still a minor. Which means her mother has every right to not only know what she is doing, but have a say in what she is doing.

The Snake Pit is no place for a sixteen-year-old girl. Neither is drinking nor smoking weed."

"Who said -" I held up my hand to stop Aaron.

"I've talked to people at the Snake Pit. You've been there. Often. With Tina. And your other friends, Stewart and Carla."

I paused a beat. Aaron didn't say anything. We established he couldn't bullshit me.

I asked him about Stewart and Carla. Aaron reluctantly gave me their last names and addresses. Stewart Valentine and Carla Travis. Stewart lived in Chestnut Hill. Carla in Dorchester. Both attended a parochial school in Boston. The same school Aaron, and Bobby, had attended.

With that information, I needed to address the unpleasant topic of Bobby's death.

"I also know about your friend, Bobby," I said.

"Sucks," Aaron said. "But Bobby was a junkie."

It did suck. A young life wasted.

"His boss told me Bobby had been clean for a year."

Aaron shrugged. "Hard to stay clean."

"Were you two close?"

"We hung some in high school. Met up again with him a few months ago. But I wouldn't say we were close."

I nodded. What Aaron said about Bobby rang true enough.

"That how you found out about the Snake Pit? Then Bobby hooked you, Tina, Stewart, and Carla with fake IDs?"

Aaron nodded.

"Aaron, the Snake Pit is a bad place. A lot of unsavory people hang out there. You probably think you're invincible. I know I did at eighteen. Maybe you even think your tough. Let me tell you. You're not."

"What's your point?" said Aaron.

"My point is you shouldn't be going to the Snake Pit. You definitely shouldn't be taking Tina there. Or any place like it. And I would strongly suggest you stop the drinking and weed."

Aaron opened his mouth. I held up my hand again. He shut his mouth.

"I get that you're eighteen. Legally an adult. But the drinking age is twenty-one. It may not make sense you could get sent to war, but can't buy a beer. But it's the law. More to the point, Tina is only sixteen."

Aaron let out a sigh.

"Lost my fake ID anyway."

Seeing as Bobby had been his contact for the fake ID, Aaron was probably on the sidelines for a while. Not a bad thing. Perhaps an opportunity to straighten himself out.

"Aaron, the Snake Pit is a place where bodies end up in dumpsters."

Aaron didn't say a word. But his eyes did a lot of talking. Recognition. More than hearing about a story on the news. A deeper recognition. Also fear.

"Is there something you want to tell me?" I said.

Aaron shook his head. "Heard about that dude on the news. Sucks for him."

Just like Bobby, it did suck for that guy. But Aaron was lying. At least not telling the whole truth. Maybe he did hear it on the news. But he already knew.

I decided to dig a little more. See how far I could push Aaron.

"Weren't you at the Snake Pit the night that guy was killed?" I said. We both knew the answer.

"Yeah," Aaron said. No point in denying it. We'd already established I had done my homework. "Left pretty early, though. Before they found the guy."

Aaron was still lying. His eyes. The lack of confidence in his tone of voice. The way he shifted on his feet.

What do you know, kid? I doubted he was involved. Aaron might be on his way to becoming a major burnout, but he didn't strike me as a killer. But he knew something.

"The police are investigating. If there is anything you might remember from that night which might help them, you should let them know."

"I don't know anything."

"If you think of anything," I said, "You could call me. I can help. Especially if you think you would be in danger."

"That's assuming I knew something that could put me in danger. Which I don't."

He doth protest too much. No doubt in my mind Aaron was lying to me. But we were done for the time being. I could tell I wouldn't get any further with him.

"Stay away from the Snake Pit. And take Tina on nice dates. Like the time you rode the Swan Boats."

I turned to leave. I paused and turned back. "Oh yeah, just say no."

"Huh?" Aaron said quizzically.

"From the 1980s. Listen, kid, stay off the booze and weed. You have your whole life ahead of you. Don't screw it up by being stupid. And definitely don't screw up Tina's life."

One last caution for Master Hurley.

"Then you and I will have a problem," I added.

Aaron nodded. I think more to get rid of me than agreement.

"Keep my card. Call me if you need to. I'm good at what I do, and I can help you. No charge."

I walked down the front path toward my car. I heard Aaron close the front door. When I reached my car Dash stood and wagged his tail. I got in and patted him on the head.

I thought about my exchange with Aaron. I was willing to bet whatever he knew, Tina knew as well. Maybe they didn't go looking for trouble, but trouble seemed to have found them.

CHAPTER 10

JAX AND MIKEY

JAX NAVIGATED THE CAR slowly through the tree-lined Chestnut Hill neighborhood. They were confident Aaron Hurley would be home. They had followed him all night long. There was never a good opportunity to approach him. Too many witnesses.

They trailed him home just after ten. They circled the block and found a convenient location to park out of sight. Jax and Mikey each took a shift watching the entrance to the neighborhood while the other slept. Aaron Hurley never left.

The two brothers waited until Aaron's parents left for work.

"Stop here," said Mikey.

"This isn't the house," Jax said.

"We'll walk. I don't want to draw any attention to the house by parking our car out front."

Jax and Mikey got out of the car and walked toward the Hurley's house. They approached from the side and moved around the back. They were careful to stay out of range of the yard's security cameras.

Mikey had taken careful note of the security system when they posed as utility workers the day before. They spent a better part of the afternoon casing the yard and taking note of Aaron's schedule. If Aaron's mother hadn't been home, it would already be over. Bought Aaron another day.

Aaron seemed to like lounging by the pool. He spent the entire afternoon by the pool until he left for his waiter job. Mikey hoped Aaron would be at the pool again. There was a small blind spot in the security cameras to gain access to the backyard. The other outside cameras watched doors and windows, not the pool area. Perfect.

Jax and Mikey had been careful. No one had seen them approach the yard. Plenty of trees and bushes to conceal them from potential nosy neighbors. Tall trees surrounded the back yard to offer plenty of privacy. More perfect.

From their spot in the bushes they had a clear view of the pool. Aaron came out of the house and flopped down in one of the poolside lounge chairs. He was a tall, skinny, kid.

Aaron wore designer swim trunks. No shirt. Working on the last of his tan before fall weather arrived.

Mikey tapped Jax on the shoulder. Time to move. The two brothers stood and pushed through the thin leafy branches of the bushes. They walked across the perfectly green and lush grass to the stone pool deck.

Aaron didn't hear or see them. Music blared through his headphones and his eyes were closed as he soaked up the sun.

"Hey, kid!" Mikey said.

Aaron opened his eyes and sat forward. He took off his headphones. He blinked at the sunlight and put on his sunglasses.

It took a moment to register, but Aaron recognized Jax and Mikey. While it had been late the other night, there had been enough lamplight in the alley to get a good enough look at their faces. These were the guys.

Aaron bolted out of the lounge chair and turned to run toward the house. Jax grabbed him by the arm and spun him around.

"Where are you going?" Mikey said. "We need to talk."

"I don't know anything."

"Then why did you try to run?" Jax said.

"I just remembered I left the stove on in the kitchen. Water probably boiling all over the place."

Mikey gave the kid credit for thinking on his feet. But they all knew Aaron wasn't fooling anyone.

"You need to be straight with us, or this will go very badly for you," Mikey said. It was going to end badly no matter what, but they needed Aaron to have hope it would be okay if he cooperated with them.

Aaron nodded reluctantly. He wished that private investigator were still there. These guys were big, but that Drew guy looked like he could take them. At least allow Aaron time to get away.

"You need to tell us if you have spoken to anyone about the other night," Mikey said.

"I don't know anything about the other night."

"Didn't I just say you need to be straight with us?" Mikey said.

Jax twisted Aaron's arm. Aaron winced.

"No. I haven't said anything. And I won't. It's none of my business."

"You are correct," Mikey said, "it isn't any of your business."

"You were defending yourselves," Aaron said. Probably not true, but he knew the situation was very bad.

"Sure," Mikey said. "What about your three friends? Have they said anything?"

"No. We all made a pact. We wouldn't say anything. To anybody. Ever."

"You all made a pact," Mikey said.

"Did you pinky swear?" Jax said with a chuckle. "Maybe a blood oath?"

Aaron's eyes flashed between Jax and Mikey. Frightened. Less hopeful than a moment ago. These guys were toying with him. They were enjoying this.

"I swear," Aaron said, "none of us will ever say a word about it. We don't want any trouble. We can't even be sure what we saw."

He paused a beat. Thinking. They weren't buying it. What could he say to convince these guys?

Aaron continued, "Whatever the reason for what happened, I'm sure it was justified. Guy had it coming to him." Was that enough?

"You're right. He had it coming to him," Mikey said.

His voice was calm. Deliberate. No remorse.

Mikey took the backpack off Jax's shoulder. He placed the bag on the lounge chair and unzipped it. He took out a pair of latex gloves and put them on.

Aaron tried to break free. Jax's grip was firm. Jax handed Aaron to Mikey.

Mikey held him as Jax put on a pair of latex gloves. He then took a handkerchief out of his pocket and wiped away any prints from Aaron's arm.

"I want you tell us the names of your three friends and where we can find them," said Mikey.

Aaron looked stunned. A deer in headlights.

"Did you not understand?" Mikey said. "Your three friends. What are their names? Where do they live?"

"I don't know," said Aaron. "Just some people I met at the Snake Pit. We had a few drinks. Smoked some weed. That's what we were doing in the alley. Smoking weed."

"I believe you were drinking and smoking weed," said Mikey. "But I think you're lying about not knowing the other three."

"Honest. I don't know their names. Besides, we were high. Our memories are cloudy. Who would even believe us?"

"Sorry, kid," Mikey said. "It doesn't work that way."

He moved Aaron toward the edge of the pool. "Kneel down," Mikey said.

Aaron locked his knees and stood still.

"Kneel or I'll knock you to your knees."

Aaron knelt at the edge of the pool. Mikey forced Aaron's head underwater for a moment. He lifted Aaron's head up.

"How about now?" Mikey said. "Are you ready to tell me what I want to know? Names. Addresses."

Aaron may have been crying. It was hard to tell with his head soaking wet.

"Hey, Mikey," Jax said. "What about his phone?"

Mikey looked at his brother. "Smart thinking, little brother. Take a look."

Jax picked up Aaron's phone. He scrolled through the pictures first. He found one of Aaron with the other three. Aaron's arm around one of the girls.

The other two teens may have been a couple.

Jax then scrolled through the contacts. He found Carla, Stewart, and Tina alphabetically by first name. Like most close friends, no last names were needed. No addresses either. Same reason.

"Just first names. And no addresses."

"What are their last names and addresses?" Mikey said to Aaron.

Aaron kept silent. He knew this didn't look good for him. He had seen what they were capable of. If he could protect his friends, he would.

"Maybe he needs some incentive," Mikey said to Jax.

Jax held up Aaron's phone showing Tina's profile picture. "She's cute," he said. "Girlfriend?"

Aaron stared down at the pool water. Mikey jerked Aaron's head toward Jax.

"Look at it," Mikey said.

Aaron looked and then just as quickly averted his eyes.

"Girlfriend or not," Mikey said. "It doesn't matter. Give us their last names and addresses or not, it doesn't matter. We are still going to find them. And we're going to start with Tina."

"No!" Aaron screamed, trying to break free.

"We're done talking," Mikey growled.

He pushed Aaron's head back into the pool and held him under the water. Aaron struggled for a time. Then stopped. Mikey shoved Aaron's body into the pool face down.

Jax and Mikey watched as the body drifted toward the center of the pool.

"Should never swim alone," Mikey said.

"Yeah," Jax said. "There are over three thousand non-boating related drownings every year."

"Really?"

"Read it somewhere."

"You read?" Mikey said.

"Ha, Ha. Very funny. So what now? No last names or addresses makes it harder."

"Don't you know I always have a plan? Let me see the phone."

Jax handed Mikey the phone. Mikey tapped out a group message to Carla, Stewart, and Tina.

THE GUYS FROM THE SNAKE PIT FOUND ME.

I GOT AWAY. BUT WE NEED TO HIDE.

MY FAMILY HAS A CABIN NORTH OF BOSTON.

Mikey provided the address to a cabin their uncle had left them. It was located in an isolated corner of a campground. They had buried bodies on the property before.

"Tell them not to tell anybody," Jax said as he looked over Mikey's shoulder.

"You're on a roll today, little brother."

Mikey went back to typing.

WE DON'T KNOW WHO WE CAN TRUST.

DON'T TELL ANYONE.

NOT EVEN THE POLICE.

THESE GUYS MAY BE BAD COPS.

I'M TURNING OFF MY PHONE.

DON'T WANT TO BE TRACKED.

I'LL MEET YOU AT THE CABIN THIS PM.

"Nice," Jax said.

Mikey hit send. As soon as the message had been delivered, he deleted it from Aaron's phone. Forensics would be able to recover it, but they'd need a reason to go looking.

Mikey placed the phone on the lounge chair.

"Do you think they'll show?" Jax said.

"Yeah. I think they'll show."

"No more loose ends."

"We never leave loose ends," Mikey said.

The two brothers removed the latex gloves, wadded them up, and put them in the backpack. They retraced their steps across the lawn and pushed through the bushes.

CHAPTER 11

DREW PATRICK

I CALLED BONNIE TO give her an update and arrange a time to speak with Tina. Preferably later in the day. Maybe Tina would be more cooperative than Aaron had been. Bonnie was in a meeting. I left her a message.

Dash and I drove back to Cambridge. I met up with a professor in Harvard Yard who was interested in my investigative prowess. His case was outside my area of expertise, but he insisted he wanted to hire me. I told him I would think about it and get back to him. I didn't hurt for cases, but neither was I in a position to turn many down. But I'd only take a case if I thought I could help.

After concluding my meeting with the professor, Dash and I took a walk through Harvard Square and around Cambridge Common. We crossed Garden Street and took Appian Way, past the Harvard School of Education, to Brattle Street. We continued along Brattle to my office building. Dash peed on his favorite bush and we went in.

State Police detectives Robert Burke and Isabella Sanchez were sitting on the bench outside my office door. Dash wagged his tail when he saw them and pulled on his leash.

"Look at the handsome boy," Detective Sanchez said.

"Dash is a real looker, too," I said.

Sanchez rolled her eyes at me and scratched Dash's head as he nuzzled up to her.

"Nice to see you, too, Detective Sanchez," I said.

She ignored me and continued to lavish Dash with attention. I knew where I stood in the pecking order.

"What's up?" I said to Detective Burke.

"Let's talk in your office."

I unlocked my office door, and we stepped in. I took off Dash's leash and hung it on the hook by the door. Dash claimed his spot on the couch. I sat behind my desk. Burke and Sanchez sat in the chairs I had in front of my desk for clients.

Robert Burke was in his fifties and had been a State Police detective going on twenty years. He was six feet and slightly overweight. His athletic build giving way to age and less exercise. Like me, he had an Irish complexion. I liked Burke. He was straightforward and committed to doing what was right.

Isabella Sanchez just made detective a year ago and was twenty years younger than Burke. She stood a head shorter than him and was in better shape. I'd only worked with her on a few cases, but I immediately liked her. Smart, tough, and honest.

"What were you doing at Aaron Hurley's house?" Burke asked, getting right to the point. He probably had a heavier caseload than I did.

"Mother of his girlfriend hired me to work a case. I went to ask Aaron some questions. Why?"

"He was found floating face down in his swimming pool," Sanchez said.

I stared blankly for a moment as I processed what Sanchez just told me. Then she continued, "Neighbor's dog got loose and went into the Hurley's yard. Started barking like crazy. The neighbor came and found the body in the pool. Called 9-1-1."

"I assume, because you are here, you don't think it was an accidental drowning?" I said.

"Made to look like it," said Burke. "Probably would have been ruled accidental if not for the rash on the kid's shoulders, neck, and arm."

"What type of rash?" I said.

"Allergic reaction to latex," Sanchez said. "Aaron Hurley had a severe latex allergy. He would break out in hives shortly after contact."

"Like from latex gloves," I commented.

"Exactly."

Like latex gloves one would wear to prevent leaving finger prints or traces of DNA at a crime scene.

"Placement of the rash would indicate he was manhandled a bit," Burke said. "Then his head shoved underwater."

"The rash is consistent with a hand firmly placed on the back of the neck," added Sanchez.

We all sat silent for a few beats. Burke and Sanchez likely joining me in thinking about Aaron's last moments. Tragic in every way.

"Crime Unit recovered some foot prints on the ground in bushes along the yard," said Burke, breaking the silence. "Two sets of prints. Both men's twelve. We have molds of the prints, but I'm not sure it will tell us much if they are common shoe brands."

"So we're looking at two suspects. Males. Likely at least six feet tall each," said Sanchez.

"Doesn't exactly narrow it down too much," I said.

"But it's a start," Sanchez said.

Burke then said, "We got the media to hold off on the story until tonight. We don't want to spook either the kids or alert whoever did this. What do you know?"

I told them what I knew so far. Including school and home addresses for Carla Travis and Stewart Vincent. I also shared my theory on how the dots were beginning to connect.

"So you think Aaron and the other three," Sanchez paused to look at her notes, "Tina, Stewart, and Carla, saw something related to Thomas Murphy's murder?"

Thomas Murphy. Now I had a name for the man beaten to death in the alley.

"Yeah," I replied. "My original theory was they had some information about the murder. Perhaps they found the body in the dumpster. With this new information, my current theory is they witnessed his murder and or the dumping of the body."

"Okay," said Burke. "It's as good a theory as any." He paused a moment. Sanchez and I waited. Burke stood and walked toward my office window.

"So whoever killed Murphy went after Aaron to keep him from talking?" Burke said as he looked out on Brattle Street.

"That's what it looks like," I said. "It would also now appear that the overdose death of an employee of the Snake Pit should be considered suspicious."

Burke turned to look at me. "Say more."

"It was ruled an accidental overdose, so it wouldn't have come across your desk. But the employee's name was Robert

Sampson. Went by Bobby. Aaron and Bobby knew each other in high school. Bobby supplied Aaron, Tina, Stewart, and Carla with fake IDs. He was found dead yesterday. I learned that when I visited the Snake Pit last night to speak with him about Aaron."

"I would tend to agree with you that is all very suspicious," said Sanchez, "but do you have anything else to go on? Sadly, death from accidental overdoses are not that uncommon."

"The manager at the Snake Pit said Bobby had been clean for a year."

"Still not much," said Burke.

Sanchez sat forward. "But given the connection to Aaron, the Snake Pit, and the timing of both deaths –"

Burke was already nodding as he interjected. "You're right," he said. "There's at least enough to look into it. The Snake Pit was already the common denominator in the deaths of Thomas Murphy and Aaron Hurley. If there is a third," Burke held it his hands apart, "I'm really liking our guys being connected in some way to the club."

Sanchez eased back into the chair. She jotted something down in her notepad.

Burke moved away from the window and sat back down.

"My guess is that Bobby Sampson's death has to do with his connection to Aaron Hurley," I said.

"Our killers figure out Bobby knows Aaron and where to find him," said Burke.

"They get what they want and dispose of Bobby as a potential witness," added Sanchez.

"And it all goes back to Thomas Murphy's murder," I said. "Aaron was in the wrong place at the wrong time. Bobby was the way to get to Aaron."

"Aaron was both killed to keep him from talking," said Sanchez, "and likely their way to locate Tina, Stewart, and Carla."

It was a conclusion we had each already come to in our own minds. Sanchez said it out loud.

"If we're right," I said, "Tina, Stewart, and Carla are in danger." Another conclusion we each had already reached. I put it out there for the record.

"Have you been in contact with your client?" Burke asked me.

"I left a voice mail message with Bonnie Ross to speak with Tina. Preferably today. I wanted to see what Tina might know that Aaron didn't want to tell me. Obviously, that was before I knew about Aaron's death. Tina will still be in school, but I'll want to go with Bonnie to get her when school lets out."

"We'll want to speak with Tina, and the others, as well," said Burke. "This is part of two murder investigations now. Possibly three, if we can find enough evidence to pursue one for Sampson's death."

"You should look hard," I said. "Given all we've discussed, I don't see how there isn't a connection."

Burke nodded in agreement.

"I'll bring Tina to speak with you," I told Burke. "Just text me a time."

"Will do," he said as he pushed himself up out of the chair.

"We'll also arrange State Police protection for the teens," Sanchez said as she stood.

I got up along with Sanchez.

Dash raised his head and hopped off the couch. Sanchez scratched him behind the ear. He knew he was irresistible.

"Not that I don't appreciate being cleared as a suspect," I said, "but why so quickly when you don't have any other solid leads? And how did you know I was at the Hurley's?"

Burke took the second question. "Your business card was in his pocket," he said. "Wet, but still legible."

"I had them printed on sturdy card stock with high quality ink."

Neither Burke nor Sanchez seemed impressed. Perhaps all my effort at having the best business cards of any Massachusetts PI was for not. I still liked them.

"Plus, you showed up on the home security system's front door camera," said Sanchez. "Aaron was still very much alive when you left."

"And I thought it was my stellar reputation for being one of the good guys."

"Didn't hurt," said Burke. "But the security footage helped." He smiled and clasped my shoulder. "Besides, you wouldn't be dumb enough to give out your business card just before killing somebody."

A partial compliment from my old friend. "Not to mention I'm an upstanding citizen and respected private investigator."

"Sure," said Burke. "I'll text you with a time to bring the Ross girl by our office."

"I love your dog," Sanchez said as she gave Dash a final pat on the head.

"He's available for walks and cuddling."

"I will have to keep that in mind," she said as she scratched Dash's ear. He thumped his tail against the floor. A Dash seal of approval.

He watched with disappointment as Sanchez and Burke left my office. Dash ran over to the window. He looked down and whimpered.

"I tried," I said to him. He looked at me and then back out the window. He did pitiful well.

I called Bonnie again. Still in her meeting. Typical mid-level management in corporate America. Meetings to discuss other meetings. I left her a more urgent message and told her the plan for meeting Tina when she got out of school.

I didn't want to alarm Bonnie, but I had no idea who we were dealing with. It was liking chasing shadows. And they were one step ahead.

It was very likely they knew about Tina. It was equally likely they would be going after her.

CHAPTER 12

"TINA IS MISSING!" BONNIE's voice over the phone was wracked with terror. "I just arrived at her school and she isn't here."

"I'll be there in a minute," I said as I went right onto Broadway off Cambridge Street. I passed the Harvard Art Museum and continued on past Broadway Marketplace and Starbucks. I pulled onto the school grounds and found an empty spot in the faculty lot.

Bonnie was waiting for me near the school entrance.

"What do we know?" I said.

"Tina went with a group next door to the Cambridge Public Library to do research for a city history project. When it was time to come back to the school for dismissal, Tina was nowhere to be found. Drew, what if they? . ." Bonnie's voice trailed off, and she choked back tears.

"We're not going there," I said. "It is unlikely that is what happened."

"How can you be so sure?"

"Experience. The time required for our bad guys to find Tina, specifically when she was in a different place than she normally would be during that class time. There are also too many witnesses."

"So, what then? Tina left on her own?"

"That's my guess. Maybe she somehow found out about Aaron's death and freaked."

"His death hasn't been on the news yet," Bonnie said.

"My gut is telling me Tina left on her own. Most likely with Carla and Stewart. I don't know," I paused a beat. "Maybe Aaron didn't respond to texts or phone calls. They probably suspect something is wrong."

"Because they figure those monsters are after them?" Bonnie said as she stared into the distance.

"Where might Tina go?"

Bonnie shook her head and said, "Under these circumstances, I don't know."

"Any relatives or family friends she might turn to?"

"Maybe my parents. But they live in California."

"California is pretty far from Massachusetts. It wouldn't be a bad place to run to."

"They would have called me if Tina had contacted them."

I nodded. But we needed to be certain.

"Call them and check."

Bonnie took out her cell phone. I looked over toward Cambridge Public Library. People entered and exited. Books to borrow. Books to return.

People moved along Broadway. Some walked. Some biked. A woman stood on the sidewalk checking her cell phone and then glancing up at approaching cars. A Toyota Camry pulled over. A purple Lyft amp glowed from purple to green. The woman got in the car.

"Tina hasn't contacted them," Bonnie said.

I looked at her and said, "Does Tina ever use Lyft or Uber?"

"Sometimes. When it is more convenient than taking the T."

I saw a small glimmer of hope in Bonnie's eyes. A glimmer we detectives get when we realize a clue.

"Everything happens through the phone app," I said. "Can you access her account?"

"Not directly," Bonnie said. "But the charges go on my credit card."

She was already using her credit card app to check for any recent transactions.

Finance at our fingertips.

She looked up from her phone with a slight smile. "Tina took a Lyft just before school ended."

I called Burke.

"I was just about to call you," he said. "Did you pick up the Ross girl?"

I told him what happened. He told me both Carla and Stewart were nowhere to be found either. Burke agreed with my theory that the three teens had taken off together. He said he would find out Tina's destination.

"Detective Burke with the State Police is pulling the record for Tina's ride," I said to Bonnie after I hung up with Burke.

"So we wait?" Bonnie said.

"Once we have an address," I said, "we get Tina and back to our plan of getting you two to the State Police safe house."

Bonnie had a look of cautious optimism on her face. I felt better than I had before knowing Tina took Lyft somewhere. But I wouldn't be okay until Tina was in the safe house. I'd seen too many cases go sideways to be satisfied with the present situation.

CHAPTER 13

TINA HAD TAKEN LYFT to Vincent Auto Sales. The car dealership was owned by Stewart Vincent's brother, James. Or "Jimmy Sells for Less" according to his advertisements. A good bet we were right about Tina, Carla, and Stewart being together of their own free will. I felt reasonably sure they were borrowing a car and getting out of town. Dash could have sniffed that one out.

I hoped we weren't too late. If they had already left, I hoped Jimmy knew where they were headed.

Burke and Sanchez met us at Vincent Auto Sales. I had also called Jessica. If I needed to take off after the teens, I wanted her riding shotgun. No one better to have with me if we ran into trouble. Not to mention I liked spending time with her.

Burke asked Bonnie to stay in my car. Jessica offered to stay with her. She would have a calming affect. Another of her many wonderful qualities.

"What car can I put you in for less?" Jimmy said as we walked into the showroom of shiny new cars.

"I'm Detective Burke, this is Detective Sanchez," Burke said to Jimmy as they flashed him their badges.

Jimmy looked at their badges and then glanced toward me. I shrugged my shoulders. No skin off my nose if Burke didn't want to include me in the introductions.

I knew I would take a back seat when law enforcement was involved. I was once the guy who made private investigators take a back seat. Didn't mean I liked it now that I was a PI, but I played along.

"Has your brother, Stewart, been here today?" Sanchez said to Jimmy.

"Is he in trouble?"

"He could be if we don't find him," Burke said.

"I don't understand," Jimmy said. If he knew what was going on, he hid it well. Of course he was a car salesman.

"We don't have time to explain," Burke said gruffly. "Has Stewart been here today?"

"Yeah, he was here. With his girlfriend, Carla, and another girl. They left about fifteen minutes ago."

"Did they take one of your cars? Do you know where they went?" Sanchez said.

"I gave him the keys to a Ford Escape," Jimmy said. "It's one of my used cars. He asked if he could borrow a car for a weekend trip to New Hampshire. That's all I know."

"Color? Year? Tag? VIN?" Burke said.

Jimmy thought for a moment. "Navy Blue. I'd have to look it up for the other details."

"What are you still standing here for?" Burke said. "Get us that information."

Jimmy retreated quickly to his office. He returned a few minutes later with the details.

"The car also has LoJack," Jimmy said.

Sanchez took the car's information back to their unmarked Crown Vic. She entered the Escape's details into the National Crime Database, activating the LoJack.

"Will my brother and his friends be okay?"

"We hope so," I said.

Jimmy looked at me. *Yep, I can speak.*

"We have a transmitter signal," Sanchez said ducking her head in the showroom door.

I turned and followed Burke toward our cars. Sanchez had the laptop sitting on the hood of the Crown Vic. We gathered around and looked at the map on the screen. The LoJack indicated the Escape's movement. It was heading north out of Boston.

"Maybe I should borrow the computer and go get the kids," I said.

Burke looked at me like I had said the moon was made of cheese.

"No way," he said. "This is State Police property. And you're not the State Police."

"I was an FBI agent a long time ago in a galaxy far, far away."

Burke snorted. I should have remembered Burke didn't care much for the feds pulling rank. He hated it almost as much as an uppity private investigator reminding him he once had been a fed. Despite all that, Burke and I were friends.

"Come on, Bob," I said. "You and Sanchez need to figure out who our bad guys are. I could put my considerable detecting skills on the task, but you Staties have more resources."

Burke wrinkled his forehead and his eyebrows came together. I also forgot he hated being called Bob. I didn't give him an opportunity to respond.

I said, "Our best division of labor is for me to go get our runaway teens and bring them back. I can't do that unless I can track the car."

"He has a point," Sanchez said.

Burke shot a look at Sanchez, but she was right. I did have a point. A good one. And time was wasting.

Burke picked up the laptop and handed it to me. "If you break it or loose it, it's your ass. If you tell anyone -"

"Let me guess," I interjected, "it's my ass."

"Get out of here," he said.

"Can you take Bonnie with you?" I said.

"We'll drop her off at the safe house," Sanchez said. "We already have troopers there."

I walked over to my car. Bonnie made a slight protest, but Jessica convinced her that going to the safe house was best. We promised to be back with Tina by dinner. I even offered to bring a pizza.

"No anchovies," Bonnie said trying to be upbeat.

She walked over to the Crown Vic. I handed Jessica the laptop and then got in my car. We pulled out of the Vincent Auto Sales lot and followed the LoJack signal.

CHAPTER 14

JAX AND MIKEY

JAX AND MIKEY RENTED the same make, model, year, and color as Aaron's car. They wanted the other three to see it parked in front of the cabin. It added to the legitimacy of the text. An assurance Aaron was in the cabin. That everything was okay.

Mikey paid attention to the details. He had remembered Aaron's car from them following him the night before. Even though the license plate's wouldn't match, he figured unless one of the kids was like Rain Man, they wouldn't notice something as small as that. Most people couldn't even remember their own license plate.

Jax eased the car to a stop at the end of the long dirt driveway. He cut the engine.

"Let's go," Mikey said.

Jax and Mikey got out of the car. Mikey looked around and said, "Perfect. Absolutely perfect."

The two brothers walked up the cabin steps. Mikey took the key out from under the mat and unlocked the front door. The door creaked as he opened it.

"When was the last time we were here?" Jax said.

Mikey thought a moment. "Six or seven months ago."

"Oh yeah." Jax searched his memory. "We went fishing."

"Yeah," said Mikey. "And dumped Sammy the Snitch's body in the woods."

"Sammy the Snitch," Jax said. "Poor slob."

Mikey shrugged. He stepped into the cabin. Jax followed. Mikey closed the door behind them. They sat on the couch and waited.

CHAPTER 15

TINA ROSS

TINA FREAKED WHEN SHE read Aaron's text. But she was relieved to know he was okay. She hadn't remembered Aaron mentioning a family cabin, but they had only been dating a few months. They were still getting to know each other.

She had texted Carla and Stewart right away. They agreed to meet at Vincent Auto Sales. Stewart could borrow one of the cars on the lot to drive to the cabin. Stewart made up a story they were going to New Hampshire for the weekend. They didn't want anyone to find them. None of them knew what they would do next. Maybe Aaron had a plan.

The campground wasn't very far north of Boston, but it seemed a world away. Lots of trees. A large lake, and several rivers.

The front part of the campground had a number of tent and RV sites. Rental cabins dotted the middle of the campground. They drove along a longer dirt road that split in two directions. They followed the right fork deeper into the woods. Along the way there were dirt driveways. Presumably they led to other private cabins.

"Where's Aaron's cabin?" Carla asked as they continued to pass dirt driveways.

"I don't know," Tina said. "He never mentioned a cabin to me until the text."

"Me neither," Stewart said. "But Aaron and his parents don't get along. We never spend time hanging out with his family."

They drove another mile and then Stewart announced, "I think it's this driveway."

He turned the Escape into the dirt driveway and followed it to the end.

"Must be it," he said. "There's Aaron's car."

He parked the Escape next to Aaron's car, and they got out. They went up the steps and opened the front door.

Tina froze as she looked into the cabin. Carla clutched Stewart's arm.

"Hi kids," Mikey said. "Remember me?"

He stood from the couch. Jax had gone out the cabin's side door and came up behind them, blocking any attempt to run.

"Where's Aaron?" Stewart said, trying to sound brave.

"With the State Police Medical Examiner," Mikey said.

"You bastards!" Tina yelled.

"Feisty," Jax said. "So was your boyfriend just before the end."

"Come on," Mikey said, "we're going for a hike."

Jax and Mikey zip tied the teens' hands behind their backs.

"Screw you," Stewart said.

"You think you're a tough guy?" Mikey said. "Showing off in front of the girls?"

"Untie my hands, we'll see who's tough."

"Get moving."

Mikey shoved Stewart down the front steps. He tilted his head for Tina and Carla to follow. They did. What other choice did they have?

Tina figured they would look for an opportunity to escape. If they couldn't, Tina knew the three were going to die out there.

CHAPTER 16

DREW PATRICK

WE MADE UP TIME BY exceeding the speed limit. We figured the kids were safe, but I didn't want Bonnie worrying a second longer than she had to. I also was thinking about the pizza I promised to pick up for dinner.

The Escape's LoJack led us to a campground north of Boston. I had camped there once with my family when I was a kid. It was our first and last camping trip. None of the Patrick clan took to staying overnight in the woods.

"The car is near the back the campground," Jessica said. "There are privately owned cabins back there."

"Sounds like you've been here before."

"Once or twice," Jessica said. "Before we met."

"Care to say more?"

"No."

"Woman of mystery," I said.

"The information is irrelevant to our relationship."

Jessica never took her eyes off the laptop screen. "Follow the road to the right at the fork," she said.

"Calling it a road is a stretch," I said. "More like a long dirt path."

"Well, then follow the long dirt path to the right at the fork."

I followed to the right. I glanced to the left. "The road not taken," I said philosophically.

"We go to the end and then turn right," Jessica said.

We followed the LoJack signal to the Escape parked in front of a cabin. There was another car parked there as well.

I didn't like it. We had company. And I doubted they brought dessert.

CHAPTER 17

WE APPROACHED THE CABIN using trees for cover. Jessica peeled off to the back. I moved onto the cabin porch as quickly and quietly as I could. Where was the Harry Potter Cloak of Invisibility when you needed it?

I peaked in through a front window. The cabin was empty. I went around back to Jessica.

"A lot of ground to cover," Jessica said looking at the deep woods.

"What would you do?" I asked.

"I'd follow the hiking trail. Private cabins, unlikely to come across anyone else."

"And then?"

"The trail narrows along a ridge."

"Easy to make it look like they slipped and fell," I said.

We were silent as we followed the hiking trail at a fast pace. If we were right, we needed to catch up to them before they reached the ridge.

My mind raced as we ran along the trail. *How did these guys find them? Who are they? How are we going to take them out?*

Questions and more questions. Maybe there was a more logical explanation. The cabin belonged to a friend, and it was the friend's car? Possible. But all my years of experience gave me an accurate feel for these situations. We weren't dealing with a fourth friend.

I was scared for Tina, Carla, and Stewart. I was right to be scared. Jessica's feeling for these situations is at least as good as my own. And she never even suggested other scenarios.

We knew what we were running towards. I only hoped we could get there in time and come out on top.

Jessica slowed and held up her hand. We both stopped. Jessica pointed through the trees.

A guy was positioning himself to take a leak on a tree. His back was to us. He was an inch or two taller than me. Six three, six four. And broad shouldered. Arms and legs as thick as the tree trunk he was reliving himself on.

I looked around to see if I could see anyone else. I tapped Jessica on the shoulder and pointed toward a clearing to our left. Tina, Carla, and Stewart were sitting on the ground. Hands behind their backs. They appeared unharmed. I wanted to keep it that way.

A man equally as large as the guy marking his territory stood over them. He was looking at the teens, but aware of his surroundings. He'd be hard to sneak up on.

"We're close to the ridge," Jessica whispered. "This is our best chance."

I nodded, considering our advantages.

They didn't know we were present. They were partially separated. One of them had his back to us and was otherwise occupied.

The element of surprise gave us the slight upper hand.

Best odds we were likely to get.

Jessica and I did a lightning round of *Rock, Paper, Scissors* to see who got Sir Pees A Lot. I lost. Jessica went with paper to my rock. Paper covers rock. But try telling that to every paperweight in the world.

I waited for Jessica to move into position. We agreed on the count before we separated.

Our timing had to be perfect. The two goons were likely armed. If we didn't immobilize them at the same time, someone could get shot. Especially since Tina, Carla, and Stewart had no idea of the plan.

I counted in my head. I reached our agreed upon number.

Jessica and I moved at the same time.

I crashed into my guy as he zipped up his fly. He face-planted against the tree, then staggered backwards.

Led Zeppelin's *Dazed and Confused* came to mind. Although I think the original writing credit belongs to American singer-songwriter Jake Holmes.

I spotted Jessica out of the corner of my eyes as she round house kicked the other guy. He was no doubt seeing stars as he dropped to the ground like a fallen tree. Timber!

My approach took a little longer, but I was counting on the same result. I moved in.

My opponent swung wildly, trying to figure out which vision was the real me. I always aimed for the one in the middle. I'm not sure if this guy had a similar strategy. Maybe he and his friend always made sure they were in complete control of a situation. Not today.

I focused my energy into an uppercut which popped the guy's head back. He wobbled like a drunk, but didn't fall. He clumsily reached behind his back. Clumsily or not, I couldn't risk him getting a gun.

I grabbed his arm and twisted. I heard the snap, and he cried out in pain.

I spun him around and pushed him onto the ground. I dropped to my knees and leaned into his back with all my weight. I lifted the gun out of his pants waste and cuffed his hands.

I looked over toward the clearing. Jessica was standing over the other guy. He was also face down with his hands cuffed behind his back. I smiled.

"She's like Black Widow," Stewart said as I approached.

I wondered if that made me Captain America. I didn't dare ask. My track record with the teen set hadn't been stellar on this investigation.

I cut the zip ties off Tina, Carla, and Stewart's hands. They rubbed their wrists and stood.

"She kicked his ass," Stewart added.

"Sorry I missed it," I said. "But I was busy taking out the other equally large man."

Tina, Carla, and Stewart looked at me. Not very impressed with my effort after watching Jessica's fists and feet of fury take down a guy six inches taller and almost a whole person wider than herself.

Yes, she was as close to a real life Avenger as they came. I still thought I could make my case for being Captain America. At least Batman.

After the initial euphoria and adrenaline wore off, it sank in for the three teens how lucky they were. We didn't need to tell them how close they came to dying. They knew.

They knew these two men killed Aaron. They also witnessed the two beat a man to death in an alley behind the Snake Pit.

Tina broke down in tears. The weight of it all too heavy to carry any longer. She was about as far removed from Taylor Swift concerts and shopping at the mall as she could be.

But it was over. She could make different choices. They all could.

CHAPTER 18

NORAH JONES WAS SINGING *Come Away With Me* on my MP3 player as I tossed a salad at my kitchen counter. A pan of Chicken Parmesan and a pot of Angel Hair pasta were almost ready to be plated. I wasn't much of a chef, but Chicken Parm with pasta and a tossed salad was one meal I could do well.

Dash sat at my feet watching as I tossed the salad. He guarded the floor against any piece of lettuce, carrot, or cucumber that might fall. No doubt he was also exercising every bit of his patience waiting for the piece of chicken I had cooling on a plate for him.

"More wine?" Jessica said.

"Yes, please.

Jessica topped off each of our glasses of Sangiovese. She said that Italian red wine paired well with Chicken Parmesan. I took her word for it because she knows wine. I was happy with Two Buck Chuck from Trader Joe's, but I liked the Sangiovese.

I tossed Dash a piece of lettuce. It disappeared in a matter of seconds.

"Is there anything he won't eat?" Jessica said.

"Probably not. I've stopped him from eating some pretty gross things."

"I don't even want to know."

"Smart," I said. "Especially just before dinner."

"It smells wonderful," she said.

"Can you take the salad to the table?"

"Sure."

Jessica picked up the salad bowl and placed it on my kitchen table. I prepared the plates for our main dish. I placed the two plates on the table, and we sat.

Dash whined as he looked up at the counter.

"You forgot Dash's chicken."

I got up from the table and placed the plate of cut up chicken on the floor for Dash. He was finished before I sat back down.

"How is Tina doing?" Jessica said as she cut into her chicken.

"Much better," I said. "She is back to hanging out with her friends we spoke with at the mall. She's off the booze and weed. Her grades are back up."

"And emotionally?"

"She's had counseling for PTSD from witnessing Thomas Murphy's murder and the ordeal at the cabin. Also finding a way to deal with Aaron's murder. It's a process, but Bonnie says she is making real progress."

"How about Carla and Stewart?"

"Burke tells me they are doing okay. They were more heavily into drinking and drugs than Tina, but both are in recovery. The whole experience was enough to scare them straight."

"I would think so," Jessica said as she forked a piece of chicken. A string of cheese hung from her fork to the plate. She twisted her fork to roll the cheese up neatly like she was pulling in a fishing line.

"Well?" I said after Jessica took her bite.

"Tastes as good as it smells and looks. You should branch out."

"Because you're sick of my Chicken Parm?" I said.

"Because you show promise in the kitchen."

Jessica smiled at me. Then she continued, "And it would be nice to have something other than Chicken Parmesan. As much as I love it."

Jessica smiled again. She could launch a thousand ships.

We talked about the case against Jax and Mikey Crane. Tina, Carla, and Stewart testified to witnessing the two killing Thomas Murphy. Pete and others at the Snake Pit were able to corroborate Jax and Mikey had been at the Snake Pit that evening just before the time Murphy had been killed.

The brothers were facing life in prison, so they ended up confessing to also killing Aaron Hurley, Bobby Sampson, and several others related to a number of unsolved cases. Their neighbors were stunned to learn Jax and Mikey were ruthless criminals and killers. Gwen Crane was devastated by the news. Her family rallied around to the financial support she needed. Neighbors looked in on her and helped with transportation to doctors appointments.

"Thank you, again, for your help," I said to Jessica.

"I'm always there when you need me."

"I know," I said.

"And you are always there for me," she said.

I nodded and smiled.

I raised my wine glass and said, "To being there for each other."

Jessica joined in the toast by raising her glass and offering me a broad smile. If we could harness the wattage of her smile, we could power all of Boston.

"To being there for each other," she said.

We drank our wine as Norah Jones serenaded us with the Ned Jones and Hoagy Carmichael song, *The Nearness of You*.

The moment was about as perfect as they come. Such moments provide purpose and meaning in my life. Another is helping people like Bonnie and Tina Ross. It is why I am a private investigator. I chase shadows so others don't have to hide from them.

**Did you enjoy this Drew Patrick crime thriller?
Please consider leaving a review[1].**

Join my Newsletter[2] for book releases, FREE stories, and more.

**And be sure to read *Shattered*[3],
the first novel in the Drew Patrick series.
Turn the page for a preview of *Shattered* >>**

---

1. https://www.jasonrichardsauthor.com/books/chasing-shadows/chasing-shadows-reviews/

2. https://www.jasonrichardsauthor.com/vip-readers-newsletter-booklinks/

3. *https://www.jasonrichardsauthor.com/books/shattered/*

PREVIEW OF SHATTERED

CHAPTER 1
Mr. Mercado

RAIN POUNDED THE WINDSHIELD, and the wipers worked overtime as Mr. Mercado drove the Hummer H2 along U.S. Route 201 in Maine. He had the road to himself on the rainy night. But he wouldn't for long. He was quickly closing in on his target.

Mr. Mercado would have plenty of time to think about the task at hand as soon as he spotted her car. For the time being he thought about the beaches, swimming holes, camping, and boating so popular in Kennebec and Moose River Valley. Mr. Mercado once kayaked in the area.

When he was a boy, his parents took him leaf peeping along the Old Canada Road as Route 201 is also known. He was innocent then. Mr. Mercado had not been innocent for a long time.

As he traveled south, he followed the old river trading routes along the Kennebec River. Mr. Mercado once killed a man who lived near the river's source of Moosehead Lake. He then thought of another body he had dumped where the river empties in the Gulf of Maine. His current hit wouldn't even require him to get out of the Hummer.

Mr. Mercado considered the young woman as she drove not far up ahead. The picture he had been given was of an attractive young woman in her twenties. She had soft features and vibrant eyes. Soon those eyes would be empty.

He wondered, do the eyes of the dead look empty because the soul has departed? Mr. Mercado didn't like to think about the soul. If he had one, he didn't think anything good would come of it when he was dead.

Mr. Mercado had done many bad things in life. He was about to do another in completing the job he had been hired to do.

Mr. Mercado could not have asked for more ideal conditions for his assignment. He played out the news report in his head: *Boston socialite loses control of a car on a stormy night and plunges to her death*. It would be ruled as nothing more than a tragic accident. It was what his client wanted.

Tail lights blurred by rain appeared ahead. Mr. Mercado pressed on the accelerator to get closer. The car was a small sporty model. It's Massachusetts license plate matched the letters and numbers he had committed to memory.

Mr. Mercado pressed the gas pedal to the floorboard and felt the power of three hundred and ninety-three horses as the Hummer's V8 engine roared. The front grill of the massive SUV quickly closed in on the bright tail lights of the young woman's car. Mr. Mercado felt the bump as all 6,614 pounds of his ride slammed into the rear of the unsuspecting sports car.

The car swerved before its driver regained control. Mr. Mercado sped forward once again. The Hummer slammed harder into the back of the car and the car fishtailed on the slippery road. Mr. Mercado pressed the Hummer forward and made contact with the car as it spun out of control.

With that final push the sporty model slid off the road and went over the edge. Mr. Mercado continued driving as he heard the crash and explosion. He glanced into the rearview mirror as a fireball lit the night sky. Drops of rain captured the orange glow.

The Hummer's wipers swept away the hard rain as Mr. Mercado continued along U.S. Route 201 toward I-295. He once again had the rode to himself. Mr. Mercado thought about the job that awaited him in Boston.

CHAPTER 2
Drew Patrick

"ARE YOU A SERIOUS DETECTIVE Mr. Patrick?" asked Cynthia Holland as she considered my office. She paid no attention to my Beagle-mix, Dash, as he slept in his corner of the couch. Surprisingly, Dash showed no interest greeting her when she entered the office. He had looked at her and then went back to sleep. His reaction told me a lot.

Cynthia Holland's eyes rested on the Red Sox bobble-heads on my desk.

"Give-away nights at Fenway Park," I said. I tapped the bill of the hat on the Mookie Betts doll and its head bobbled. "Arriving early can have its perks."

"Yes," she said, "I suppose it can." She tried to force a smile. Or maybe it was gas. Hard to tell.

Cynthia Holland looked like she needed reassuring, and I needed a case, so I answered her as seriously as I could muster, "I'm a former special agent with the FBI." I tilted my head toward my diploma from the FBI Academy, which hung next to my Bachelor of Science degree in Criminal Justice from Northeastern University. Perhaps those pieces of parchment would offset the bobble-heads.

Cynthia Holland shifted her dark eyes toward my office wall as she looked at the framed diplomas. Her eyes scanned like an x-ray machine. I wondered if she thought they might be fakes. She then looked at me without blinking.

"I know full well you were with the Federal Bureau of Investigation, and now you own this detective agency," she said.

"I even have my name on the door," I said. "And business cards printed on heavy stock."

She frowned, and I wondered if I blew being serious. I waited a moment and then she sat down in one of the client chairs opposite my desk. My keen powers of observation told me she was staying. A regular Sherlock Holmes.

"Can I get you anything to drink? Water, coffee, or tea?" I said.

"No, thank you," she replied.

I sat behind my desk and gave her my best GQ smile. She did not smile back. Maybe it had been gas earlier.

While lacking in warmth, she was not an unattractive woman. I guessed she was in her early 50s. Cynthia Holland was thin, of average height, and had a perfect complexion and expensively styled shoulder-length brown hair. She was exquisitely dressed in a knee-length skirt and matching blouse from a designer boutique.

She placed a Gucci purse on her lap and rested her hands on top. She probably needed to rest her left hand throughout the day given the size of the diamond ring on her finger. Cynthia Holland looked me directly in the eyes and let out a deep sigh.

"My husband should be here any moment," she said. "We'll wait until he arrives to begin."

"Sure thing," I said. I flashed another of my winning smiles. No reaction.

My mother always told me I had a nice smile. Maybe it wasn't true. I made a mental note to ask her later.

Being a private investigator I'm accustomed to long stretches of silence. But those usually occur when I'm alone on a stake out, not sitting in my office with a potential client. We were past the normal lull in conversation and well into an awkward silence.

It didn't seem to bother Cynthia Holland. She sat expressionless. Maybe she was meditating. Or maybe it was relief from the possible earlier gas having passed.

I doubted another smile would help. I thought about whistling a nice tune, but I wasn't confident we had the same taste in music. Given her reaction to the bobble-heads, I didn't think talking about the Red Sox winning the world series was a topic we had in common.

"Hello," a man's voice said from just outside my open office door.

I looked up and Cynthia Holland turned around. Dash hopped down from his spot on the couch, stretched, and trotted over wagging his tail. Cynthia pressed herself deeper into the chair as Dash walked past her.

The man was two or three inches shorter than me at around five eleven or six feet. He was lanky with a perfectly tailored blue pinstripe Brooks Brothers suit, crisply pressed white shirt, with French cuffs, and a light blue domino patterned designer tie. He had neatly trimmed short brown hair, parted on the side.

I spotted a gold Rolex watch on his wrist as he reached down and scratched behind one of Dash's floppy ears. My investigative prowess told me this guy was the source of Cynthia Holland's diamond ring.

"You're late, Jeffrey," she said.

Bingo! Drew Patrick, detective extraordinaire.

"Sorry," he said, "I wasn't sure where on Brattle Street the office was located."

Cynthia Holland rolled her eyes. If Jeffrey noticed, he gave no indication.

I stood and offered my hand. "Drew Patrick."

"Jeffrey Holland," he said taking my hand and shaking it. "Pleasure to meet you."

"Likewise," I said. "Please, have a seat," I said as I indicated the empty client chair next to the one occupied by his wife.

Jeffrey Holland leaned over and offered her an awkward peck on the cheek. Then he sat in the chair. Dash resumed his position on the couch and went back to sleep.

"How about the Sox?" Jeffrey said as he eyed the bobble-heads.

"Alex Cora had a masterful first season as Manager," I said. "Perfect complement to a team of talented players."

Jeffrey Holland nodded in agreement. Cynthia Holland rolled her eyes again.

"Can I get you anything to drink?" I said.

Jeffrey shook his head. "No, thank you."

"Now we can begin," Cynthia Holland announced.

I placed a notepad in front of me and grabbed a pen, ready to take notes like a seasoned journalist. Or at least a half-decent private investigator.

"Mr. Patrick, we would like to hire you to find our daughter," said Cynthia Holland.

There was nothing in her tone which suggested the seriousness of a missing daughter. None of her behavior since entering my office would suggest I would hear anything like what she had just said.

Jeffrey Holland leaned forward in his chair. "This has happened before," he said. "Ashley will go off for a few days and not tell us. She won't respond to texts or phone calls and then show up again."

"Last month she jetted off to Paris for a long weekend," said Cynthia Holland. "Was incommunicado for three days. Came back with shopping bags from Hermes."

"She bought me this tie," said Jeffrey Holland as he lifted up the end of his tie. He looked at a moment, lost in thought.

"If your daughter is prone to flights of fancy," I said, "why the concern now?"

"She has been gone five days," said Jeffrey Holland. I detected concern in his voice. "Ashley has never been gone more than four days before without any form of contact."

I nodded my head.

"Have you gone to the police?" I said.

"No," Cynthia Holland said. "We don't want this in the media. Imagine the embarrassment when she turns up after a trip to Europe or the Caribbean."

"I can certainly take your case, but the goal is to find your daughter. The police can help."

"We'll take that into consideration," Jeffrey Holland said.

"Do you know where she may have gone?" I said.

"Not a clue," Cynthia Holland said.

"Actually," Jeffrey said, "she mentioned something about a lake house up north."

Cynthia Holland whipped her head in her husband's direction. "Why on earth would Ashley tell you and not me?"

Jeffrey Holland shrugged. He probably knew, or had a strong opinion on the matter, but I didn't blame him for wanting to avoid a confrontation with his wife.

"Do you know where up north?" I said. "New Hampshire? Vermont? Maine? Canada, even?"

"No, I'm sorry," said Jeffrey Holland. "Ashley didn't say where."

"What about her friends? Have you spoken to them?"

"The ones we could reach didn't know anything more than we do," Jeffrey Holland said.

I asked more questions to try to establish the best profile on Ashley I could. I also had the Hollands text me Ashley's picture and give me her detailed description, information on the car she drove, and contacts for known friends and associates.

We went over my daily rate, plus estimated expenses, and Jeffrey Holland wrote me a check to cover my first day. I'm sure he spent more on monogrammed hankies.

The Hollands didn't strike me as the most loving parents, but they did come to me find their daughter. And even less than stellar parents can know when something is not right with their kids. The fact the Hollands decided to hire a private investigator meant we were in that territory.

I would do my best to find Ashley. I've done this enough times to have confidence in finding her. I only hoped she would be okay when I did.

CHAPTER 3

I spent the rest of my morning contacting people on the list the Hollands had given me. None of those conversations generated any leads. What they did do was confirm Ashley was very much a free spirit. Her friends didn't seem particularly concerned about Ashley spending four days out of contact with anyone.

While possible the Hollands hiring me would turn out to be unnecessary, I didn't think so. My detective's intuition told me they were right to be concerned. I just needed to figure out my next course of action.

Since I always work better on a full stomach, I determined lunch was in order. It would give me time to think through the case. And since two minds are better than one, I contacted Jessica Casey to join me.

Jessica worked as a private investigator for a large international detective agency based in Boston. She had a snazzy office in their downtown building and mostly dealt with high-end clients like the Hollands. I only occasionally got high-end clients, and that was fine by me.

"Hello, handsome," Jessica's voice greeted me when she answered her phone. Jessica and I are romantically involved, but we haven't found a need to label our relationship. What we have is special, and it works.

"Join me for lunch?" I said.

"I have an afternoon full of new client meetings, but I can sneak out for a bit. In fact, my first meeting is in Cambridge. I can meet you somewhere in Harvard Square."

"How about Pinocchio's?"

"Ooh, big spender."

"Your afternoon of new client meetings limits our options. Besides, what could be better on a cool fall day than a hot slice of Sicilian-style pizza?"

"Just one slice?" she said.

"Okay, two. Maybe three."

"I could go for a slice of eggplant."

"Now why would you go and ruin a perfectly good slice of pizza by adding eggplant?" I said.

"I like eggplant. You should expand your palate."

"I'm good with pepperoni."

"At least we can agree on no anchovies," she said.

"Definitely," I said.

"Give me a half-hour," she said. "I'll meet you there."

"I'll be the good-looking guy with a hint of danger about him."

"I just happen to go for good-looking guys with a hint of danger about them."

"Lucky me," I said. And I was.

CHAPTER 4

Harvard Square was buzzing with activity as people enjoyed the beautiful fall afternoon before rain from northern New England would roll in later. I pulled my Harvard baseball cap on tightly against the crisp autumn breeze. The crimson cap, with the white capital H on front, gave the appearance that I was a person of great intellect. Or that I had shelled out twenty-four bucks at the Coop.

My gray Northeastern University sweatshirt represented my alma mater and kept me toasty warm as I walked down Brattle Street. Perhaps my sweatshirt confirmed the authenticity of my college diploma for Cynthia Holland. My blue jeans were classic Levis and well broken in, just the way I liked them. The same went for my New Balance sneakers.

I passed Brattle Square and crossed over Mount Auburn Street. I cut through Winthrop Square and admired the bright fall colors on the trees. I crossed John F. Kennedy Street to Winthrop Street. Harvard students passed me on the sidewalk carrying pizza boxes from Pinocchio's.

Through the plate-glass window I could see the small pizza and sub shop was busy as usual. I went in, made my way to the counter, and ordered. Two slices of pepperoni for me, and a slice of eggplant for Jessica. I completed the order with a Coke and bottled water and paid. Jessica would sip her water while I had a Coke and a smile.

Two coeds got up to leave and offered me their table by the window overlooking Winthrop Street. I smiled and thanked them. They smiled back. The usual reaction. Maybe I didn't need to check with my mother.

I placed the plates of pizza on the table and went back for the can of Coke and bottled water. As I was sitting, I spotted Jessica on Winthrop Street approaching the restaurant. Her five foot eleven inch athletic frame moved quickly. Jessica believed in arriving at least ten minutes early to any appointment. Even for a casual lunch with her favorite guy.

As she entered Pinocchio's, customers did a double-take. I saw it often. At first glance Jessica had a passing resemblance to Gisele Bündchen. With a little closer inspection the customers realized Jessica's hair was more chestnut, and she had light green eyes.

A few took a moment longer to consider her. Could Gisele be in disguise? Is there a Tom Brady sighting? All the patrons of Pinocchio's seemed satisfied Jessica was not Gisele and went back to eating their pizza and subs.

"Do people ever wonder if I'm Tom Brady when I'm with you?" I said.

Jessica wrinkled her nose and said, "You have dark hair and are two inches shorter. But you have similar blue eyes."

"You left out every bit as handsome and a similar gun for an arm."

"Goes without saying."

"But that would be a 'no'?" I said.

Jessica nodded her head and then gave me a kiss.

"But you're the star quarterback of my team," she said as she removed her blue LL Bean fleece pea coat.

"Best team around," I said.

Jessica placed her jacket over the back of her chair and sat. If she hadn't already told me, she would be meeting a client, her charcoal pants suit and white blouse would have been a clue.

Everyone at Jessica's agency wore suits. Partly their clientele, and partly the detectives were former FBI, police, and lawyers. Jessica fell into the latter category.

"So Pinnacle Detective Agency doesn't have enough clients in Boston that they are sending you to Cambridge?" I said before taking a bite of my pizza.

"Worried about the competition?" Jessica said with a grin.

"We don't exactly fish in the same client pond," I said. "Unless the Pinnacle waters are drying up."

"Hardly," said Jessica. "Some of our clients have us on retainer to investigate the missing keys to their beamers."

"Can't they just take the Mercedes instead?"

Jessica paused in taking a bite of her pizza and laughed.

"And you wonder why I don't have you over to the office more," she said grinning.

"Oh, I know why," I said. "Plus I hate to wear suits."

"How did you ever last five years with the FBI?"

"I was finding myself," I said.

I polished off my first slice of pizza. Jessica was only halfway through her slice.

"Seriously," Jessica said, "we have some very challenging cases. Plus there is all the travel."

Jessica often spent time in New York, Los Angeles, London, and cities across Europe.

"Ah, the glitz and glamour of international investigations," I said. "You know, if you ever want to take on grittier cases, Dash and I can always make space for you on Brattle Street."

"While we work well together on the occasional case, I'm not sure being partners, professionally speaking, is in either of our best interests."

"Does save on changing the sign and business cards," I said.

I was well into my second slice. Jessica still had a quarter of her slice remaining.

"Besides," she said, "I get enough grit when I help out on some of your cases."

"A little grit can go a long way," I said. "Although I may be stepping up in the world."

"Do tell."

"I reeled in a rather large catch this morning," I said. "I'm actually surprised they didn't go to Pinnacle."

"Maybe they did, and we didn't take their case." Jessica looked at me playfully.

"Or they decided to go straight to the Commonwealth's number one private investigator."

"Who is the client?" Jessica said. "I can tell you if I met with them."

"It's a good thing you are so cute," I said.

"Right back at ya," she said, raising her bottled water and titling it in my direction.

I raised my can of Coke and took a sip. "I can't believe they ever messed with the formula," I said.

"That was over thirty years ago," Jessica said.

"It was a big deal at the time."

"Tell me about your new client."

"Cynthia and Jeffrey Holland," I said. "They've hired me to find their daughter, Ashley."

"Wait a second," Jessica said. "Ashley Holland? Do you have a picture of her?"

I pulled out my cell phone and found a picture of Ashley the Hollands had sent me. I handed the phone to Jessica. She considered the photo of Ashley a beat, then nodded her head.

"The luck of your Irish family may truly be working for you today," she said. "Ashley Holland is a subject in one of our investigations."

CHAPTER 5
GRANT WORTHINGTON

THEY WERE HAVING DINNER at the Polo Lounge of the Beverly Hills Hotel, the epicenter of Hollywood celebrity dining. Where you sat mattered for the occasion you were celebrating.

Grant Worthington had his favorite power booth for when he closed one of his high profile movie deals. Tonight, Grant selected an alcove for an intimate date.

Victoria looked ravishing in a long-sleeve silhouette Herve Leger Nathalia Signature Essentials Dress. She certainly had the legs and curves to pull off the mid-thigh and form-fitting outfit. The cultured pearl necklace perfectly accented the black dinner dress and her long dark hair.

Victoria took in every inch of the room's hunter green walls and striped ceiling of white and the same hunter green. Celebrities and other Hollywood elite sat comfortably at tables covered in fine white linens and set with understated silverware, glasses, and white coffee cups. She drew in the scent of the simple flower arrangement at the center of the table.

Grant gazed into Victoria's hazel eyes which sparkled in the glow of the candlelight. He flashed a smile and his perfectly polished teeth glistened. Grant wasn't the best-looking guy in town – not by a long shot. But he made up for his below average looks and average build by wearing Armani suits, Rolex watches, and driving Bentleys, Lamborghinis, and Ferraris.

It also didn't hurt that he was one of the most powerful producers in Hollywood. Grant Worthington could either make someone a star or kill their career with a phone call.

Victoria hoped Grant would make her a star. Grant hadn't yet told her it was never going to happen. He hesitated because the sex was simply too good.

"So, my darling, what will it be tonight?" Grant asked.

"I'm thinking a McCarthy salad to start, and the Crispy Seared Branzino for my entrée."

"Excellent choice."

"Let me guess what you are having," Victoria said. "Polo Crab Cake, followed by Filet Mignon."

"You know me so well," Grant said as he placed his menu on the table. "What about dessert?"

"I thought I was dessert?" Victoria said playfully.

"Of the best kind," Grant said. He reached across the table and took Victoria's hand. "I booked us the Presidential Suite for the evening."

"You spoil me," said Victoria.

"Nothing but the best, my dear. Nothing but the best."

They raised their glasses of Dom Pérignon.

"To us," said Victoria.

"Yes," said Grant. "To us."

As they clicked glasses, Grant momentarily wondered what his wife might be having for dinner at their home in Boston.

CHAPTER 6
EVELYN WORTHINGTON

EVELYN WORTHINGTON turned her Diamond Metallic White Mercedes-Benz S 560 off Sunset Boulevard and pulled to the front of the Beverly Hills Hotel. She handed her keys to the valet and walked past the pink columns and stepped onto the red carpet leading to the hotel entrance.

Evelyn had made this same walk countless times over the past thirty years. But no one was likely to recognize her in the blonde wig and colored contact lenses, making her eyes appear blue rather than their natural brown. She had purchased a Christian Siriano Grass Green Slip Dress, which she would wear just this once.

Mrs. Grant Worthington had swapped out her her diamond engagement ring and gold wedding band with an equally stunning blue sapphire gemstone set in fourteen karat white gold. Attention to details mattered when you wanted to go unnoticed by even those who know you best.

Evelyn passed through the grand lobby and headed directly to the Polo Lounge. Grant thought he was so clever, but Evelyn was always a step ahead of him. He thought she had stayed behind at their home in Boston to attend to some of her charity work there.

Evelyn entered the Polo Lounge knowing Grant had reserved seating in an alcove for intimacy – for *his date*. Yet she knew the spots in the Polo Lounge where you could see everyone without being seen. Attention to details.

CHASING SHADOWS

From her perfect vantage point, Evelyn watched and waited. She ordered a glass of white zinfandel and scrolled through pictures on her phone. The private investigator she had hired sent her all the evidence she needed of Grant's affairs.

Grant had taken two lovers over the past year. Tonight's bimbo would be his third.

How dare he? Evelyn thought as she swiped through one picture after another. Grant dining in the finest restaurants, staying in five-star hotels, and giving *his lovers* lavish gifts.

Fine dining, fancy hotels, and lavish gifts were expressions of Grant's love and affection Evelyn once received.

Thirty years, she thought. *Thirty years we have been married. I was with Grant when he was a nobody. The only woman who would have him before he ruled Hollywood.*

Evelyn and Grant had met in college back in Boston. He was one of the least attractive men she had ever laid eyes on, but he was smart, funny, and charming. Evelyn would often tell her friends she could "see the beauty within." With her above average looks and smarts, Evelyn could certainly have dated any other guy. But she was drawn to Grant.

The two fell in love and were married two weeks after graduating college. Neither wanted children. Another selling point in Evelyn's book. No, Mr. and Mrs. Worthington were going places together.

Grant inherited a small fortune in old Boston money and bankrolled his windfall into a movie studio. He had always dreamed of making it big in Hollywood.

Too ugly to be a movie star. Not creative enough to direct. But Grant had money, a knack for spotting talent, and the ability know what the public wanted to see before they knew it themselves.

Evelyn was a shrewd businesswoman and kept both the studio's and their home's financial affairs in order. At least half of their fortune was owed to Evelyn's money sense. The Worthingtons had spent thirty years building an entertainment empire.

Now Grant was screwing around.

Evelyn hated his cheating.

But she still loved him.

Despite his cheating, Evelyn still loved the homely jerk.

There had been some pretty good years the past three decades. She wanted to rekindle the magic. But his cheating – his lovers – stood in the way of their happiness.

Evelyn slammed her phone down on the table. A little too hard. She attracted glances from other diners. Some of them the most notable stars in Hollywood.

"Is everything alright?" asked a waiter.

"Yes. Sorry. Everything is fine."

She had lost her cool and attracted unwanted attention, no matter how little or fleeting. She wouldn't let anything like that happen again. Attention to details mattered.

Evelyn ordered a Caesar salad, Scottish salmon, and another glass of white zinfandel.

Still no sign of Grant and the little bitch he was currently boning.

They'd arrive soon, she had no doubt. Grant would want to leave enough time for screwing in the hotel room he had booked here at the "Pink Palace."

Enough time for dinner, sex, and to go home and pretend none of it happened.

"Just another day at the studio," he'd say. "Another power meal at the Polo Lounge making the next big movie deal."

Yeah, right, Evelyn thought. *Just another day, my ass.*

Evelyn finished her salad and was starting on the salmon when in walked Grant and the twenty-something piece of eye candy. She was a younger and prettier version of Evelyn.

If Evelyn were being honest, the images on her phone didn't do the young woman justice. She was stunning.

No doubt Grant was letting her believe she would be the next big name in Hollywood. She likely was nothing more than great in bed.

Evelyn no longer could match the looks, but she was certain she knew more about pleasing Grant in the sack.

Why, Grant? Evelyn thought to herself. *Why am I not enough?*

Evelyn watched as Grant led the little whore to their table. Her arm looped through his. Her lithe body moved gracefully. Evelyn was certain the form-fitting black dress had Grant turned on. Hell, Evelyn was almost turned on.

"Why do you do this to yourself?" Evelyn said quietly. "Why torture yourself more than you have to?"

Evelyn didn't have an answer. All she knew was she needed to be there.

She needed to see with her own eyes.

It was the same with the other two. The beautiful young blonde with the perky breasts. The handsome young man with the dimpled chin. That one surprised Evelyn.

Not that she judged. Frankly, she didn't care the sex of the people Grant slept with. She only cared that he was sleeping with them.

Light conversation filled the room.

Waiters delivered orders.

Grant and *his date* smiled and laughed.

Evelyn watched as the two toasted with their flutes of champagne. After dinner they would rush to one of the suites or bungalows.

"I hope it's worth it," Evelyn muttered in the young woman's direction.

Evelyn knew one thing for certain: by getting into bed with Grant, the young woman had sealed her fate.

End of Preview
Get your copy of [1]*Shattered*[2]

---

1. https://www.jasonrichardsauthor.com/books/shattered/

2. https://www.jasonrichardsauthor.com/books/shattered/

REVIEWS

CAN YOU DO ME A BIG favor and take a few minutes to leave a review of *Chasing Shadows* on your favorite book e-retailer?

Reviews are very important in establishing the all important "social proof" when readers are deciding what to read next. Having a certain number of quality reviews are also required for me to promote my books through many of the book promotion sites.

Thanks for considering leaving a review. I really appreciate it. Even if you don't leave a review, thanks for reading this story!

Leave a Review[1]

---

1. https://www.jasonrichardsauthor.com/books/chasing-shadows/chasing-shadows-reviews/

VIP READERS NEWSLETTER

Join my VIP Readers Newsletter[1]
to get FREE stories, exclusive content, new release alerts, and more.

---

1. https://www.jasonrichardsauthor.com/vip-readers-newsletter-booklinks/

BOOKS BY JASON RICHARDS

Read [1]*Shattered*[2] the first novel in the series.

For a complete list of my books visit:
https://www.jasonrichardsauthor.com/books/

---

1. https://www.jasonrichardsauthor.com/books/shattered/

2. *https://www.jasonrichardsauthor.com/books/shattered/*

SHORT STORIES BY JASON RICHARDS

I TYPICALLY RELEASE a short story between each novel. They are fun, quick, reads. I like to call them Short Thrills. I send my short stories for free to my newsletter subscribers[1] as a 'thank you' for being loyal readers. They can also be purchased at book e-retailers.

For a complete list of my short stories, visit:
https://www.jasonrichardsauthor.com/short-stories/

---

[1]. https://www.jasonrichardsauthor.com/vip-readers-newsletter-booklinks/

ACKNOWLEDGMENTS

I WOULD LIKE TO THANK you for taking the time to read what I write. None of this would be possible without my readers. THANK YOU! It is also true that a writing project does not come into existence without the help of others. I want to thank my editor Lois for her dedication to making what I write better. A big thanks to my family and friends for their unending support, especially to my wife and our son.

ABOUT THE AUTHOR

JASON RICHARDS IS THE author of the Drew Patrick detective crime thriller series. As a young boy he loved the Hardy Boys mysteries and then graduated to Sherlock Holmes. He was firmly hooked on detective stories as his favorite fiction genre.

As a teen he discovered the tough and witty Spenser by Robert B. Parker. As an adult Jason found another favorite in the Elvis Cole novels by Robert Crais.

He loves creating the characters and world of the Drew Patrick novels and hopes his readers enjoy being part of the journey.

Jason is married with a teenage son and a Beagle-mix dog (the inspiration for Dash).

Printed in Great Britain
by Amazon